Brain-damaged America

The Novella Experiment, Volume 1

William Leigh

Published by A Fictional Dog, 2024.

This is a work of fiction. Similarities to real people, places, or events are entirely coincidental.

BRAIN-DAMAGED AMERICA

First edition. September 13, 2024.

Copyright © 2024 William Leigh.

ISBN: 979-8227960207

Written by William Leigh.

Brain-damaged America
Prologue

It all started with the clocks acting up; running in reverse, taking an hour to tick off a minute, refusing to tick at all. This quickly escalated to time itself, its very gradual - one might almost say timeless - fading out. A state of confusing non-time ensued, everything seemingly stuck in sticky place. The classic, if somewhat clichéd, condition of *no time like the present* turned out, at least in the minds of an increasingly apprehensive public, to potentially equal infinity. Hardly anyone understood infinity, which made it all the more terrifying. People suddenly trapped in the middle of doing things, from waving goodbye to starting to cry to preparing to die.

But then a brief reprieve: Time wasn't the problem, we were informed. It was entropy. You know, the process of ever-increasing disorder in a system? Oh right, entropy. Of course, but who needs that, anyway? Turns out we do; a lot, in fact. Life as we know it requires a healthy, fully functional entropy. When entropy goes wrong, or in this case decides to make an extremely ill-advised U-turn, time just can't work properly. Life begins to unravel. The various possibilities of things become not only impossible, but inconceivable. No way around it, yet all happening so slowly that no one noticed it for what felt like forever.

Needless to say, this cosmological screw up became the fodder of countless conspiracy theories. A seemingly bottomless pit of conspiracies raging in the brains of countless idiots, but no way to get them out. They began to stagnate and stink, as brains slowly atrophied in skulls. Until, that is, the whole telepathy kicked in. Apparently we were all telepaths, we just didn't know it. So much we didn't know. We didn't even know that we didn't know. Outside time, as we vaguely recalled it, our minds had nothing to do. The erosion of entropy, and subsequent loss of all that new - and yes, truth be told, mostly worthless

- information a normal entropy guaranteed, created a dangerous vacuum. And then somewhere in the midst of all this slow-moving misery a switch got switched, a toggle toggled. The dumbest ideas were set free to seek out the path of least resistance. The conspiracies began to flow, from brain to brain, and we tended to wholeheartedly believe each and every one of them. And the irony of it all: the more delusional the mind of the telepath, the more powerful its ability to telepathically influence others. Think of it as the universe giving humanity that long overdue middle finger.

Only a matter of what used to be called *time* before somebody came up with the ... *it has to be aliens behind the whole thing* idea. And then there it was in everybody's head. The fucking aliens had messed up entropy and ruined time. We all knew it to be true. From their secret bases on the dark side of the Moon, they had spent a thousand years planning Earth's invasion. Fuck up entropy, stop time, conquer Earth with zero resistance. But they hadn't worked out all the possible consequences. Suddenly they were facing a rather small planet covered in what would eventually be seven to eight billion dead bodies; an enormous clean-up operation, even for a technologically advanced species. The invasion plan was abruptly cancelled.

We all cheered, soundlessly, in our slowly dissolving heads. We had defeated a superior alien race. Or at least so went the story making the rounds through the shattered minds of people who no longer knew what or even how to think.

The vast majority of conspiracy generators were indeed seriously disturbed and equally vacuous imbeciles. They prayed to a horse-faced demoness with fake blonde hair and the grin of a long-term mental patient, going by the name of Mallory Malaise Brine. Not the brightest bulb in the basket, but with a certain flair for convincing her mostly brain-dead constituents that she was the answer to all their dimwitted desires. She employed a now fully weaponized social media with the twisted savvy of a digitized savant; spreading lies, deceptions, insane provocations, the continuous call for insurrection. With each incendiary posting she included a snapshot of herself in bikini (*not for the faint of heart*), or mildly out of focus underwear shots (*thank god for blurriness*), or her on horseback, her face and the horse's virtually indistinguishable, or, on rare occasions, fuzzy naked pics, both herself and the horse, wearing nary a stitch. She timelessly amassed fifty million followers. The whinny became their war cry.

Desperate for the next unhinged thing to do, these far-right numbskulls began a search of every mine shaft in the country, intent on locating and exposing the so-called Deep State. They assumed the nefarious liberal agenda was alive and well somewhere far underground, controlling both the warp and the woof of a fractured nation. The end of time, they reasoned, was a leftist conspiracy. Subvert the will of the people by breaking all the clocks and watches. The radicals were clearly in cahoots with the aliens.

And all of this was, relatively speaking, merely the beginning; before the onset of the blathering epidemic, the rumors of the Lizard People uprising and - saving best for last - the attempted reanimation of former President Ronaldo Rumpus, a.k.a. The Don, from within his Floridian crypt.

One

Jane and Jenna are just about to sit down for supper when the sirens go off. News to them that the town even has sirens. The usual warning for an approaching tornado, of which there are an ever-increasing number, is an old man on a bicycle blowing a whistle. No telling how many old men, unable to out-pedal the whirlwind, have already been lost. So yes, a case could be made that the sirens were at least theoretically saving elderly lives, but this did nothing to lessen their irritating shrillness.

And all of this happening before the arrival of Jane's mother, June - a shrill irritation in her own right - due for a mealtime get-together, complete with coming out announcement for dessert. Jenna and Jane have been living together for a year, ostensibly as strictly platonic best friends. This is a far as they dared go, residing as they are on the outskirts of Rabid City, Oklahoma, where the rules are rarely bent, never broken. Particularly those courtesy of God himself. There is, apparently, not even a single reference in the Bible to lesbian lovemaking.

Jenna goes to a front window to investigate, observes a very large group of people walking slowly down the street; a silent procession of the dispossessed, each of them holding what appeared to be a cell phone, or Smartphone, if you prefer, the absurdity of that misnomer as it applies to this particular group notwithstanding.

What is it? Jane inquires, busy trying to call someone about having the sirens turned off - or better yet permanently disabled.

Best guess, a parade of the undead, Jenna replies.

Not another zombie movie, I hope, says Jane.

Except this is real life, Jenna says.

Real life? Jane wonders. She has her doubts.

They appear to be in some sort of trance, says Jenna.

As long as they're not gathering in front of our house, lighting torches, says Jane.

And the lesbian witches of Rabid City shall be dealt with in the harshest possible terms.

Jane walks to the window, standing next to Jenna. What do you think they're doing? she asks.

Could be one of those rightwing rallies, suggests Jenna.

Possibly, says Jane, but then shouldn't they be screaming racist, anti-Semitic, homophobic epithets?

In that instant the throng of Rabid humanity abruptly stops, all of them tilting their heads back, gazing up at the evening sky. A collective *aaaaaaah* is released from a multitude of mouths.

What the hell are they looking at? Jane wonders.

Maybe it's the first time any of them has noticed the moon, says Jenna.

I may have an obligation to go outside and investigate, says Jane.

Jane, it turns out, is a police officer. A gay female cop existing in a repressive - to the point of painful cliché - male cop's world.

Aren't you off duty? Jenna asks.

An officer of the law is technically never off duty, says Jane in her official-sounding voice.

Even when she's in bed, with her lover, her lips busy exploring the contours of another woman's body? Jenna wonders.

I'm not entirely sure about that, Jane admits. Let's call it a gray zone.

If only we had decided to go to bed before this began, Jenna says.

Jane muses: Only to risk June arriving, ostensibly for a meal, seasoned with no small amount of excruciating conversation, then discovering us in bed, naked, in the throes of unholy passion.

She imagines the following scenario:

June, who never knocks first, enters the bedroom at the exact instant Jane's mouth is due to arrive on her 'best friend' Jenna's vagina.

Jane's original intention had been to employ the much more erotically charged *C* word, only switching to the more neutral *V* word at the sound of June's footsteps just outside the bedroom door.

June is in total disbelief at what she's seeing; can only assume that her daughter has decided to switch careers, from police officer to gynecologist. And isn't a mother always the last to know. Still, she can't quite understand why a vaginal exam would be occurring at 7:30 in the evening, in Jane's bed, no less, or why both patient and doctor have to be naked.

She attempts to formulate a question, the answer to which might clear at least some of this up, but nothing materializes. There are, it seems, no words. Maybe there never have been any. She stands there, in silence, watching for what feels like forever.

It did feel like forever, says Jenna.

Tell me about it, Jane says. I've never had my mouth poised in such proximity to a vagina for that long in my entire life.

So we're definitely going with vagina now? Jenna asks.

Well, with my mother standing right there ...

Yeah, that makes sense, I guess. By the way, where is your mother now?

Jane looks around. I have no idea, she says. Wait, has she even arrived yet?

If she hasn't, Jenna says, who was standing in the bedroom doorway earlier?

Were we in the bedroom earlier? Jane asks.

If we weren't, says Jenna, why would someone stand there so long watching us?

Jane tries to recall where she left her service weapon. Maybe we should search the house, she suggests.

Hold on, says Jenna, something doesn't feel right.

Only something? Jane asks. I'm thinking more like everything.

What if none of this has even happened yet?

So, then, where are we?

I'm not sure. Maybe we should go upstairs and ... you know.

Fine, but this time I'm keeping my gun under the pillow.

Two

Dave Darwin, the B.S. News Network's head anchor - *not to mention number 2 on People Magazine's list of Incessantly Annoying Talking Heads to Keep a Wary Eye on* - has just finished his pre-show prep, including the application of an appropriately wise and understanding cyber gel face, when he is handed an urgent news update. He scans it with eyes as wide as the gel residue, not yet completely dry, will permit.

What the fuck is this? Dave wants to know.

Just in from an assortment of the affiliates, Candace, his assistant, replies.

Verified? Dave asks.

Several of our quasi-reliable sources do appear leaning towards confirmation.

Oh for Christ's sake, Dave snorts. Just give me the bottoms up, babe.

Candace winces imperceptibly at Dave's use of the word *babe*. They report what may be mass screaming, howling in the hills, hordes of disoriented humans spouting mostly pure gibberish, she informs him.

Did you at least push them for details? Dave wants to know.

Naturally, says Candace. But at that point, in each case, our sources lapsed into incomprehensible gibber jabber themselves.

Dave sighs, at the same time making the *hmm* sound. We'll need more, he says. Who do we have in the field?

Candace puts an index finger to her chin. Uh, I believe Cynthia's out there, somewhere.

This time Dave makes the *uggh* sound, a look of intense distaste stretching the cyber-seals around his mouth. Why does God hate me? he asks no one in particular.

Several possible reasons come to mind, but Candace choses to hold her tongue. There are after all rules for dealing with the *great* Dave Darwin. Never gaze directly at his latest artificial face; always wear something that highlights both breasts and buttocks; never engage in discussion concerning his former wives, his current girlfriend, the astronomical cost of a pack of cigarettes and, of course, God. Acceptable topics for conversation: the size of his penis, oral sex, his sheer brilliance, the enormity of his bank account, the importance of his role as not only the dispenser of truth, but also later day prophet to the news-hungry masses.

Cynthia Cumberbatch, Dave hisses. The big ass bitch from Boise.

Pretty sure she's from Bismarck, says Candace, immediately wishing she hadn't.

Dave glares at her. Purses his artificial lips, as if to issue a stern warning regarding contradicting the star of the show, or, worse case, pronounce Candace fired, possibly adding something along the lines of, you'll never work in network news again, honey cheeks.

But I'm probably wrong about that, she quickly adds.

Dave nods. Suppose there's no helping it, he says. Get her on the line. We'll lead with the Mid-West madness.

Will Candace mention that all reports of the strange phenomenon have thus far come out of Texas, Alabama, Mississippi and the Florida Panhandle? Do we even have to ask?

Mid-West Madness, she repeats. Love it!

How soon to air time? Dave shouts.

We're live in fibber fobbering fish sticks, one of the set techs answers.

Whaaaaa? Dave screeches, sensing something seriously wrong with his mouth. The words inside it are bumping around, haphazardly dribbling out across his lips in slow motion.

Wa da flick is happy-run? Dave wants to know, but no one is quite sure what he means.

Car -dance, he screams. Whore is yowl?

Candace, meanwhile, having made her way to the women's restroom, now squatting on the floor, staring at her watch. The spinning dials have lost all meaning. She is terrified, mesmerized, mortified. She imagines herself sitting on one of the toilets, her pants and underwear down around her ankles. She begins to urinate, feeling oddly soggy and uncomfortable. She hears Dave's bellowing, wonders if she should answer, and if so, what an appropriate response would be?

She takes a deep breath, shrieks. Beast paddy tic Inuit.

Scoliosis, Dave howls back. Sickly wit syllogisms.

Three

Burr Greensong reacquires a semblance of consciousness at the intersection of Thrall Street and Vivian Way, just outside downtown Hypocrisy. He finds himself in a throng of slow-moving folk, their arms lifted heavenward, voices piercingly raised, singing: *Our eyes have seen the coming of the great malignant howl, it is clawing at our scalps and burning in our bowels.*

Burr wonders how he has come to be here, seemingly involved in an activity that, on the face of it, makes absolutely no sense.

He nudges the person beside him, an obese gentleman with bushy clumps of white hair protruding from both nostrils.

Excuse me, Burr says, but what is going on here?

The man glares at him with crusty-looking, opaque eyeballs. We follow the fiddlefaddle, the man says.

The ..?

The flume, the night of screams, the unclean underwear.

Burr wonders if his hearing has somehow become impaired.

We are of the battalion of the Brine, her whiskered mane, her holes of pain.

Wait, says Burr, are you talking about Mallory Malaise Brine?

The mass movement ceases, a chant rising up, *Brine ... Brine ... Brine...*

Burr gazes down at his feet. He is not wearing any shoes. When he looks up, the large face of a woman is directly in front of him. He cannot detect a body. Merely a giant floating head.

Where is the rest of you? he asks the looming face.

The entropic cannibals are among us, she says. Keep watching the sky.

The sky?

The lie, the pie, bye the bye ... we all die.

Die did you say? Burr asks.

The face answers with a sigh.

But when?

Tis nigh.

The face floats off. Burr remembers his phone. He begins searching his pockets. Yes, he says, extracting it from the right front pocket of his pants. He taps the green phone icon, presses home. It rings.

And rings.

Finally, a sleepy female voice.

Burr? Is that you?

He doesn't recognize this voice. Uh, yes.

Where the hell did you go? she asks.

I ... uh ... may I ask who this is?

Are you drunk?

Was he? I'm not exactly sure.

One minute we were about to have sex, says the voice. The next you were running out the door, screaming like some lunatic.

I heard the calling of the wind.

What?

The wail of the three million witches.

Any chance you're having a psychotic episode?

Did you say we were about to have sex?

I'm lying here naked right this minute. Wanna guess where my right hand is?

Attached to your right arm?

Fucking dating sites. Never again.

Sorry, says Burr. Do you know anything about entropy?

Buzz-feed Bürgermeister, big boy, she replies.

Buzz what now?

Your sloping shingles, these temporal tasty cakes, this shantytown in shambles.

Hold on, think I've got it, says Burr. You're touching your vagina, right?

Brine, Brine, ain't she fine, someone screams in his ear.

Finer than the state of Carolina, someone else hollers.

But definitely not as fine as my vagina, the voice on the phone says.

Don't go anywhere, says Burr. I'll be there in ten minutes.

Yeah, yeah, at which juncture you'll dine on nothing but bloody recrimination and stale regret.

Just one thing, he says, where exactly are you?

In your apart, Mister fart.

And, uh, where is that.

Sixth and Sycamore, as far as I recall.

And where might that be?

An hour outside Black Lake, Idaho, would be my best guess.

Idaho?

By high speed train, of course.

What the ..? Hey, says Burr to the guy directly in front of him.

The man turns, his face appearing melted; no eyes to speak of, a nose drooping down towards his mouth, upon which a twisted smile appears frozen in perpetual mockery.

Where are we? Burr asks.

On our way to the Ark.

The Ark?

Haven't you heard the good news? Noah's death sentence has been commuted.

This place, I mean.

Oh, says the withered mouth. This place.

Exactly.

On the outskirts of paradise, of course. Or possibly purgatory.

I mean which state, says Burr.

The great state of Uncertainty.

Yeah, putting it mildly.

Tell me, ghost boy, says the mouth. Have you supped on the various apertures of our Holy Sister-in-Law Mallory?

Four

Mallory Malaise Brine, recently emerged from the shower, stands naked in front of the floor to ceiling mirror admiring, if not her beauty, of which, admittedly, there is little, but rather her feistiness. Yes, she is a feisty, born again misapprehension, conceived under a twisted conjunction of deranged sociopaths. Both virgins at the moment of conception, and in that instant they knew that penises were not simply for making pee pee, vaginas not exclusively for their monthly exudation of Christ's holy blood.

I am the blood messenger, Mallory reputedly had shouted at the moment of her birth.

She had then looked back at her mother's ravaged genitals, and instantly knew the wicked wages of copulation.

I love this illusion of ugliness, she tells her reflection. God loves it too. He spoke to me in a dream once. Or was it a trance? Or possibly at a high school dance?

She begins to do a little jig, her eyes glued to her smallish breasts, the somewhat overgrown patch of dark brown hair between her legs. She turns, gazing over her shoulder at her ass. The ample ass of a real woman, she thinks. Not the tight little ass of some skin and bones anorexic slut. Some lefty radical vegan whore. She has the ass worthy of the Lord's caress. Who needs the tiny, uninspiring hands of her husband (technically ex-husband), when Jesus himself has the holy hots for you?

She knows, of course, that the aliens are watching, not to mention the sky lasers of the Israelites currently aimed at her house. Let them thrash and threaten, leave their forged postcards in her mailbox, reputedly from still-living American voters, wishing her all the best, tied to a burning stake in hell.

She lets go a loud whinny at her reflection.

She is impervious. A rock of alternative truth. Unhinged fury in the guise of rightwing recidivism.

And once the excavation of the sarcophagus of King Don is complete, she will become invincible; strolling through the halls of power on the bones of irrelevant middle-of-the-road whiners.

The phone rings. Mallory decides to answer it in the nude.

Malaise Brine, she rasps into her pink Smarty-phone.

Mall? A woman's voice drawls. It's me, Laura-loo Bobsmart.

Loo Loo? What a sinister surprise.

You're so sweet.

What can I do for you?

Just wanted to say sorry for calling you a psycho mudslinging menace the other day.

Oh, it barely registered, you shilly-shallying sister of Satan.

So glad we could arrive at a mutually agreeable outcome on this.

And while we're on the subject, sorry I put forward that motion to have you stripped and flayed alive by the male members of your caucus.

Just between you and me, I was kind of looking forward to it.

You always were a glutton for punishment, Loo Loo.

Which, contrary to what's all over the Internet, does not include anal sex with horse-like hung Muslims.

Thank God for the ban.

Amen to that.

Well, gotta run.

Well, me too. What's on the agenda?

Stopping by the pedophile pizza parlor protest, then harassing some teenagers who apparently don't believe in guns.

How absurd. I'm holding two of my favorite guns as we speak.

Just make sure you don't accidentally shoot yourself in that giant-sized ego of yours.

And you make sure not to get run over and horribly disfigured by a truck full of Mexican illegals.

Once the Don is reinstated, says Malaise Brine, Mexico will be no more.

Not only will he destroy Mexico, he'll make them pay for the heavy ordnance, says Laura-loo.

They're all going to pay.

But not us, right?

Did I mention, Laura-loo, that I'm naked?

I sometimes secretly think about you that way.

Really? Too bad we outlawed homosexuality.

Come on, Mallory. Part of the fun is in breaking the law.

You really are a wicked little slut, aren't you?

So my wealthy, generously-endowed, not entirely bad-looking husband tells me.

Mallory Malaise grinds her teeth. Later, Bobsmart.

With an insane smile. Up yours, too, Brine.

Five

This is B.S. Breaking News!

Good evening. I'm Bright Silversperm, here in The B.S. News studios, filling in for Dave Darwin, who, for reasons not entirely clear, has suddenly become even more incomprehensible than usual.

And now this back-breaking story!

A crowd estimated at over one hundred thousand has descended on Times Square, arms raised, chanting the melodies from several pop hits from the 1960's. Our correspondent, Rude Withers, is at the scene ... or would that be on the scene?

Whichever, says a voice in his headset.

Great, at or on the scene. Rude, what can you divulge to our mostly brain-dead audience?

Again, the voice in his headset: *Never again refer to our audience as brain-dead. Correct it!*

Uh ... a moment ago, I misspoke. What I actually meant to say was *our audience of brains well-fed.* Rude, you still with us?

I sure am, Bright, and believe me, the scene here is something out of a horribly under-budgeted sci-fi disaster movie. I, myself, have just spent the last fifteen minutes humming the melody to *Mrs. Brown You've Got A lovely Daughter.*

A minor classic if ever there was one, Rude.

Ironically, I actually dated a Betty Brown in high school, or, in other words, Mrs. Brown's daughter.

Positively serendipitous. So Rude, getting back to this let us say highly unusual event, if I may call it such, what else can you tell us? Any insights, possibly demands from the crowd, casualties thus far?

Well that's the strange thing, Bright. I mean strange in the context of ever-increasing strangeness.

Of course.

I mean, how strange can it possibly get?

I guess only that word I suddenly can't remember will tell.

You're so upright, Bright. Anyway, informed sources have, uh, informed me that this crowd is here simply to stare up at the giant clock atop this building, which houses, among other things, the world famous Hermione Greengold Theater.

So can we perhaps assume it has something to do with what clocks are supposed to do, whatever that might be?

Ordinarily, Bright, that's more or less precisely what we'd be vaguely assuming.

I sense a but on its way, Rude.

How well you know my butt, Bright.

Sorry?

The thing is, if we can just tilt our camera upwards, towards the top of the building ...

The image is a tad fuzzy, Rude.

The point being, Bright ...

Yes ..?

Are you seeing this?

Not in the least.

Well, long story short, there is no clock atop this building, housing, among other things, the world famous Hermione Greengold theater.

No clock, you say?

The top of this building is both unremarkable in every conceivable way and absolutely clock-free.

Strange, Rude, to say the least.

Excuse me, Bright, but are you saying I'm strange? Me, the strange one?

I was actually referring to the situation, Rude.

And then some, Bright.

Could it be some kind of symbolism, or going out on a crazy ledge here, irony?

Hmm. I'd have to say doubtful, Bright. According to my sources, the entry requirement for joining this particular crowd is possessing an I.Q. no higher than 75.

Explains them letting you in, I suppose, eh, Rude?

I'm not in, Bright, merely covering an event comprised of a whole bunch of not very smart people.

Right, of course. Any idea where this march to the giant non-existent clock got started?

I did ask one of the organizers about just that, Bright. Get this: Kick off point was the eastern side of the former Brooklyn Dodgers' Bridge, lower level.

That's a new one.

Tell me about it.

Shame about the Dodgers, though. I mean, what might have been had they just stayed put.

Guess we'll never know, Bright.

Well, thanks, Rude. Keep us informed.

Will do, Bright. Oh, and by the way, please give my best to Dave. Heard he may have come down with a case of the blathers.

No definite babble gabble on that yet, Rude. Whatever it is, let's just hope it's permanent.

Uh ...

Did I say permanent? Obviously meant to say post-apocalyptic.

Amen to that, Bright, and while you're at it, you can call me a red fountain pen.

All right, Rude, if you insist. You're a red fountain pen.

And you're a slippery silver slice of servitude, Bright.

By the way, Rude, have you had your blathering inoculation yet?

Don't believe there is any such thing, Bright.

So that injection I received in my left eyeball yesterday was nothing but pure Bogie?

Loved him in The Maltese Falcon, by the way, Bright. Now that's a movie you can actually sink your dentures into.

Absolutely, Rude. Just wish they had made more of an effort to explain exactly what a falcon is.

Six

The crypt itself had been constructed exactly 214.7 feet beneath the former President's Floridian estate ~ *slash* ~ golf course ~ *slash* ~ local crime syndicate clubhouse. Reportedly vast and luxuriously outfitted, it is generally regarded as *the ultimate* place to be interred, temporarily or otherwise. Upon learning of President Rumpus' apparent demise, over a million of his loyal followers began tweeting their desire to be demised as well. Whatever it took in order to join him. Whether or not Rumpus, aka The Don, was actually dead, or merely acting like a selfish little baby and hiding out until everyone started saying nice things about him, remains unclear. According to reliable sources, Rumpus had entered the lavishly equipped sarcophagus willingly. To the sheer delight of his fans, he had continued to abuse social media with his demented commentary and otherwise vile verbal drivel for over a month. At which point, the crypt went dark. Theories abounded. The Free America Conspiracy Union claimed to have clear-cut evidence that Rumpus had been snatched by aliens, taken to a planet in the Cygnus System, where he was being wined and dined nightly by members of the Galaxy's MAGA *(Make Andromeda Go Away)* Republican elite. Eventually he would be returned, equipped with new and even better ways to ruin the nation and possibly the world. Needless to say, no one but immediate family members have been allowed anywhere near the crypt. Hundreds of Rumpus' followers, however, line the periphery of the golf course each day, their phones fully charged and ready to further distort reality, in silent homage to the man who had given them the hope of a glorious return to the dark ages.

Don ... Don ... Don ... Don ... they quietly chant.

Hey, someone excitedly squeals, I've got a link to a video of President Rumpus' toilet inside the actual sarcophagus.

Everyone begins furiously web-crawling their way to the toilet link.

Imagine seeing the great man take a dump. His shit would be worth its weight in gold.

Actually, no need to make such an exchange. Ronaldo Rumpus already shits gold.

Golden turds ... Golden turds ... Golden turds ... the line of supplicants begins to chant.

Within the bowels of the crypt itself, The Rumpus' eldest son, Roscoe, has spent the better part of a day carrying in the pelts of various dead animals - some rare, some on the verge of extinction, some just run of the mill - and piling them up at the base of the sarcophagus. He pauses periodically to reminisce, visualizing the exact circumstances of each animal's final moments on Earth. As much as he enjoys his own psychopathic rants on social media aimed at his father's perceived enemies, nothing really equals the erotic thrill of the hunt. Killing things is pretty much the whole point of life, as far as he is concerned. And once his father re-ascends the throne, it will be open season, not only on all the animals, but all those who had consented to His banishment beneath the swampy ruins of what had once been the mediocre-at-best state of Florida.

Planka Moremoney, (née Rumpus), stands a short distance from the sarcophagus, her expression an admixture of disdain, revulsion and, of course, unquestionable superiority. She has always regarded her brother as a lost cause, basically an idiot, but this whole dead animal thing was compelling her to revise her opinion of him; downwards, needless to say.

You disgust me, she tells him.

Yeah, he replies, and the sight of your smug, 70% artificial face makes me want to heave.

Why are you even doing this? she asks.

As I've already told you, he says, sacrificial offering to the demon overlords is the key to successful reanimation.

Where do you get this shit?

Uh, the internet? Ever hear of it?

Uh, your head up your own ass, ever hear of that?

Little Miss high and mighty. Ever since you married that mannequin motherfucker, Morty Moremoney.

Who has more money than you'll ever have.

You sure about that, Sis? Once Daddy's back, the con will once again be on and the cash will once again come rolling in.

Daddy, as you may recall, almost destroyed the country.

And next time he'll finish the job.

Planka shakes her head, considers spitting in disgust, but remembers how Morty feels about women who expectorate in underground crypts. Then she smiles at the reminder of her impressive vocabulary.

So why am I here? she asks her brother.

Have you not seen my Facebook page?

Uh, I'd rather stick hot needles through my nipples.

Don't forget I've seen your nipples, he says, faking a yawn.

You're a pig, she hisses.

And you're a whore, he replies.

That's it, she huffs. I'm leaving.

You can't leave.

Because ..?

If you kept up with my twitter feed, the one, by the way, currently with eight million followers, you wouldn't have to ask.

Again, I'd rather be buried alive with a progressive democrat from New York.

You know, that could be arranged.

Fuck you! she screams, storming off towards the exit.

Wait, Roscoe shrieks. If we want to bring Daddy back, it's gonna require the blood of the first born daughter. No way around it.

Have you lost your fucking mind?

Oh for God's sake, Planka, relax, will you? I'm talking about a single pint, tops.

Seven

All I can tell you, Dr. Mellmack, is that, based on our latest analysis, we're losing entropy at an alarming and, needless to say, unprecedented rate.

That's a serious, potentially life-on-earth-ending boast, Dr. Portmanteau. Any chance you've scuttled the numbers?

Scrunched the scrotum, you mean?

Scoured the scullery maid?

Your miasma, Mellmack, is only surpassed by your belief in Maldivian mermaids.

Dear Lord, Portmanteau, it's happening to us now.

You're right, Dr. Mellmack. Could there perhaps be some correlation between a shrinking entropy and the increased incidence of mass aphrodisiacs?

That question actually made sense, Portmanteau.

That can't be a good omen, can it?

If only we had the time to dwell upon it with compulsive glee.

The absence of luxury should not be confused with an overall dull and dreary existence.

You may have missed your calling, Portmanteau.

You're no doubt alluding to the poet in me, Dr. Mellmack.

Actually I was thinking more along the lines of toilet stall attendant. But sure, poet could also work.

Ah, the life of a janitor poet.

Back to the issue at hand, Portmanteau.

The tissue of lies?

The shortage of toilet paper in the laboratory restrooms?

The break down of the physical universe is the initial sign of entropy's vanishing act.

Human bodies will slowly disintegrate.

The insanity of the masses will be released as a toxic vapor.

In any case, the President wants answers.

I though the President was safely locked away in his super-luxury cryptocurrency.

I refer, Portmanteau, to the current President.

Oh, right. What's his name again?

Uh, Bird ... something-or-other.

Eight

Welcome back, everyone, to the Trixie Sonnenborg Show. I'm Trixie Sonnenborg - *enthusiastic applause* - and our next guest is Professor Saul Sappershroud, a renowned expert in the fields of neurolinguistics and something called esoteric gimcrackery, whatever that might be. So, Professor Sappershroud, can you explain to our audience, preferably in terms a total idiot might understand, the precise meaning of aphasia, in particular as it relates to the ongoing phenomenon currently being referred to as the *blathers*?

Happy to, Ms. Sonnenborg.

Please, Professor, call me Trixie.

Thank you, Trixie. And may I say what a pleasure it is to be here with you today.

You're very kind, Professor.

Not at all. In fact, we often have your show on in the background, as we perform our usual magic and mayhem in the lab.

Magical mayhem does sound intriguing, professor.

Indeed.

But getting back on topic.

My apologies, Trixie.

So you were saying?

Full disclosure, some of us in the lab like to imagine you naked as we watch the show.

Oh, my goodness!

Not me, of course.

Of course.

Now where were we?

The blathers?

Ah, yes. A crude, uninformative term, but one that does cut to the chase, as we sometimes feel ourselves compelled to say.

Compelled, professor?

Peer pressure can be a bossy bossanova, Trixie.

Excuse me, professor, but is there any chance you are showing signs of blathering right now?

Doubtful, snootful, with a pout full of pitfalls.

Sorry?

You see, aphasia is generally indicative of a breakdown, usually co-extemporaneously, in either the frontal or temporal lobes of the cerebrum. Although both lobes afflicted simultaneously is not unheard of. Particularly in those restricted to the somewhat lugubrious horse latitudes.

Uh ... so something gone haywire in the old noggin knocker.

In a squirrel's nutshell, Trixie. More to the point, the sort of nonsensical speech patterns which are being evoked in the so-called blathering phenomenon reminds me a great deal of what is known as *Wernicke's Wonderbread*, generally displaying excessively long, though generally meaningless and, needless to say, predominantly white sentences.

Sounds like something we might hear from virtually any member of the current U.S. Congress.

Ah, yes. Many of us in the scientific community are hoping that Wernicke himself will soon be throwing his hat in the presidential ring toss.

Uh, according to Cindy, my real time human fact checker, Professor Wonderbread is currently 97 years old.

But still sharp as a dull scalpel. And he certainly won't be the first wheelchair-bound President.

You did mention the temporal lobe of the brain, did you not, professor?

I did, Triskaidckaphobia. Why do you thus query?

Well, Professor Suckersoot, isn't it possible that these extemporaneous time bombs being tossed about might be intimately connected to the numbskull nonsense being spouted by an ever-increasing number of high school dropouts?

Hmm, interesting theory, Trixie, you little pixie. Some hidden correlation in both speech and temporal boner displacement. I honestly hadn't considered that.

Just glad I could help.

I also enjoyed your use of the word intimately.

I'm a passionate woman, Professor, although please be advised, I rarely have sex with a first-time guest on the show.

Isn't it a pity, hums Sappershroud.

Isn't it a shame, Trixie sing-song replies.

By the way, is that clock on the wall correct?

Trixie, staring at clock. I have not the slightest idea.

How long have we been sitting here? I notice that most of the audience has either fallen asleep or left the studio.

Answer me this, professor. Did you have a beard when we began the interview?

Are you suggesting I may be gay, covering up the fact with an illegitimate heterosexual partner?

That's a scoop and half, if true.

I usually prefer one whole scoop or two. Half a scoop tends to shout uncertainty, rushing into the lavatory half-baked, as it were.

If only we hadn't thrown out the empirical method with the baby's bathwater.

I suppose you could disrobe, Trixie, and we'll see if I can win an erection.

I had no idea you were even running.

One has to these days, just to stand still. Also, I believe a stiffening penis is more in line with the sort of mental disorder to which I refer.

I, too, dream about such things. Running headlong into stiffening penises, I mean.

Ah, Trixie. How I'd like to get you back to the lab and probe all of your sumptuous, temporal-spatial orifices.

And if everything suddenly stops altogether, professor?

In that case, we'll be sitting here having this conversation til the cows come home.

Wouldn't death be preferable?

If the rumors concerning entropy are true, that option may be out of the question.

Entropy, professor?

No, nothing, mere flubber-blubber in a sea of ectoplasmic erogenous zones. Forget I said it.

Said what, again?

Entropy. Oh, crap!

Nine

I suppose I'm obligated to wonder what happened to my mother, Jane says.

Maybe the mob got her, says Jenna.

Organized crime? Jane asks with alarm. Here in Rabid City?

Or, you know, the mob outside, Jenna replies.

Oh God, Jane moans. If only I'd been a better daughter.

She never made it easy for you, consoles Jenna.

Still, says Jane, I just wish I had one more chance to say all the things I never got around to saying.

In that case, says Jenna, you're in luck.

Huh?

She's standing right behind you.

Jane gasps, spins around. Sure enough, June has somehow materialized in the living room, looking like she's just had a run in with an extremely unapologetic ghost. How long have you been here? Jane asks her.

June seems to be having some trouble speaking. I'm not exactly sure, she croaks.

Anyway, says Jane, you're probably wondering about earlier.

Earlier ... June repeats the word, showing no sign of comprehending its meaning.

Upstairs, says Jane, in the bedroom. Whatever you might be thinking you saw may not be what you actually saw.

Except it was, says Jenna.

Upstairs? June says. I don't think I've been upstairs.

Sure you were, insists Jane. Remember? Jenna and I, together in bed?

Why would you and Jenna be in the same bed? June wants to know.

Because we were making love, Jenna says.

Excuse me? June shrieks, her voice suddenly a perfect replica of the town's siren.

Don't listen to her, says Jane. She loves to kid.

What an awful thing to kid about, says June. Homosexuality is only a single step away from outright Satan worship.

Oh, we do that too, Jenna says.

You're not helping, Jane says to Jenna.

I thought tonight was the night we were going to tell her, says Jenna.

Tell me what, dear? June asks.

Jane tries to swallow but her mouth has become suddenly parched. That Jenna and I are ... thinking about getting a cat.

I'm not a big fan of cats, says June.

We're not getting a cat, says Jenna.

Jenna prefers dogs, says Jane. Can you believe it?

Actually, says Jenna, I much prefer your daughter's pussy.

I'm confused, says June. I thought you were only thinking about getting a cat.

Sorry, says Jenna, I should have used the *V* word.

Oh no, Jane, says June. Please don't tell me you're thinking about becoming one of those vegetarian people.

V, Jenna shouts, for *Vagina.*

June's eyes go all *I'm seeing that egotistical ghost again* wide, her mouth slowly opening and closing, like some politician impersonating a fish. Or possibly vice-versa.

Well, this has been fun, says Jane, but duty calls.

I don't think you should go, Jenna tells her. It could be dangerous out there.

For once I have to agree with Ginny, says June, still visibly unnerved by the whole vagina fiasco.

Ginny who? Jenna asks.

Her name's Jenna, mom, says Jane.

Whose name, dear?

Never mind, says Jane. You and Ginny just try to have fun while I'm gone.

Ten

President Birdswell sits at his desk in the oblong office, formerly oval, inside what used to be known as the White House. Until former President Rumpus had it officially changed to The Bigfoot's Lair. His intention had been to copy Hitler, a man he couldn't help admiring, but then confused The Wolf's Lair for Bigfoot's. An understandable mistake, according to Rumpus supporters; just one more example of the man's stupidity and incompetence, according to those with still-working brains and a genuine desire to stave off worldwide annihilation.

Birdswell is staring at a large pile of classified documents. In light of recent events, he is determined to not let them out of his sight. Exactly how similar *top secret* documents were turning up in his private residence, his garage, the apartment of his on-again-off-again girlfriend, even in the treehouse he had built for the kids forty years ago is not easily explained. Not that he is a stranger to things mysteriously vanishing; car keys, single socks, two former wives, those magic beans - unless that had merely been a dream - to name but a few. The case of the disappearing documents, however, has national security intrigue plastered all over it. He has gone over it in his head repeatedly, trying to work out not only the source of the leak, but also its medium. He has pretty much ruled out leprechauns in league with the opposition, primarily because every leprechaun he has ever encountered was unabashedly democrat. As the loose-lipped leprechaun Lewis had once confided in him, *I'd rather go back to being a human again, working minimum wage in a gas station in Killarney, than affiliate with any of them rightwing whack-a-doodles.*

Less easy to dismiss is the possibility that one of his many aids is also secretly moonlighting as a semi-professional magician, his or her area of expertise the old slight-of-hand, the now-you-see-it, now-you-don't, routine. So far today he has seen more aids than he even knew he had, on a variety of fairly pressing issues; from global warming and mass refugee migration, to speculation on the size of Putin's penis - by all accounts small, which would certainly explain his near-psychotic rage and uncontrollable aggression - and the appropriate placement of Abbott and Costello in the pantheon of American comedy teams.

Before him stands Major General Burton Frothmeyer, retired, his current Chief of Staff and most trusted confidant.

Any thoughts on the matter, Burton? the President asks.

Excuse me, Mister President, the matter being ..?

Who among the staff might possess magical abilities?

Hmm, Frothmeyer considers. Pamela Parsley comes to mind. She does seem to have the ability to placate the press in briefings, regardless of how riled up they are at the onset.

So you might say she's capable of putting a large, clearly disturbed group of individuals into a sort of trance. A mesmerist in our midst, in other words.

Perhaps, said Frothmeyer. But if I may ask, Sir, why do you care?

I care, says the President, because classified documents are disappearing faster than this old man's sex drive. Isn't it conceivable that each time Pamela comes in here for clarification on some issue, she is at the same time hypnotizing me? And while I'm under her spell, a few more documents mysteriously go missing?

I feel I should point out, Mister President, that Pamela is one of your most loyal staff members. She practically worships you.

Birdswell sighs. Yes, of course, that's true. Unless those republican lunatics have something on her.

Blackmail, Sir?

Just a regular email will do, Burton.

Another avenue of possibility suggests itself, Sir. One that we might want to explore.

I'm intrigued, Burton, says the President. Also, I have no idea what you're talking about.

I refer to the thing that is suddenly and inexplicably in all our heads, says Frothmeyer, his right eyebrow intriguingly raised.

Birdswell shakes his head. I can't really see how speculation on Putin's penis size is going to be of much help here.

Putin's penis is irrelevant, says Frothmeyer.

Couldn't agree more, says the President.

I'm speaking of the aliens, Mister President.

Ah, Birdswell hums. The alien menace, unseen and totally unsubstantiated, yet at the same time undeniable, for reasons that remain mired in misappropriation.

One hundred million Americans can't all be wrong, Sir.

Yes, Burton, but let's not forget the vast majority of them are stuck like angry insects in the strictly red zones.

Only until the next election, Mister President.

Not sure what we could say or do to repair all those broken brain conduits, says Birdswell.

In any case, says Frothmeyer, if we can somehow pin the missing documents on the aliens, you'll be completely off the hook.

I do like the sound of that.

So do I have your permission to get started on the appropriate spin?

The spin cycle is nobody's idea of frivolity, Frothmeyer, says Birdswell.

Nevertheless, Sir, I'm game if you are.

I do love games, says the President.

Eleven

Burr has no idea how far he's already walked. It feels like many miles, probably even more kilometers. The surge of the crowd, the smell of their confusion, the twisted ambience of their resolve. What he needs is the appearance of a train station, the only reliable means of transportation back to the start, to his apartment, where what's her name presumably awaits him still. How long masturbation will placate her, he has no idea. At some point her clitoris is bound to object, throw up the white flag, threaten to become a painful annoyance for the next week, at the very least.

All the people around him seem to have their eyes closed. Every so often the crowd stops, all heads tilted up towards the sky, arms raised, and they begin their gibberish chanting.

Mumbo mud holes and burning butt moles. In a sizzling dustbowl we feast on loopholes and rotting egg rolls.

Burr feels compelled to react to the peer pressure of the mob, also looks up, sees streaks of fiery light across the sky.

What the hell is that? he says out loud.

Alien space heaters, of course, says the old man next to him. Off to Washington, New York and all them other places where the radical rats hang their overpriced hats.

Radical rats? Burr inquires.

You know, says the man. The progressives, the ones intent on implanting all of us with control chips; and while they're fiddling with our brains, they're gonna steal all our guns, melt them down and turn them into affordable housing for illegal immigrants.

Oh, right, says Burr. Those progressives.

And President Tweety Bird, who, by the way, is some sort of robot impersonator, is the worst of the bunch.

Believe it's Birdswell, says Burr.

Say what? the man screams at him.

In that instant, the clouds above part, as if by magic, and a large luminous full moon emerges.

Wow, Burr exclaims. Look at that moon. No further reminder required of why life matters.

Where you been, sonny? the man asks. That ain't no moon.

Really? says Burr. What would you say it is?

It's called a hollow gram, of course. The work of the aliens.

Aliens, aliens, aliens, Burr mutters.

I'm this close to concluding that you is one of um, the man says, poking his almost-touching thumb and index finger into Burr's face. Don't think for one minute they don't walk among us.

Burr shakes his head, even as he can't help glancing at the people surrounding him. And what about the zombies? he whispers.

Last I heard, the man says, the zombie march is somewhere in west Texas.

That explains a lot, says Burr. I've always suspected the Texas Governor is not strictly among the living.

His name is Bud Abbott, the man snaps. Used to be part of the greatest comedy team in the entire history of teleportation. I only hope he decides to run.

For what? Burr laughs, psycho sideshow clown?

Hey, a man's background shouldn't aught to be held against him.

You're putting me on, right? Burr asks.

Let's just see if you're still laughing when my old pal Bud becomes the next Big Banana Banger of these Undercooked Steaks.

So what, super discounted meat for the masses?

And plenty of raw sausage for the deceased base.

I could definitely go for a steak sandwich.

What's holding you back? You one of them veggie vampires, or something?

Burr shakes his head, chuckling.

What's a matter, boy? Got one of them poisonous tickle bugs up your butt?

What? Wait, is that a real thing?

Real as your mamma's regret for birthing you in the first place.

You know what, says Burr, I'm going to find a different spot in the crowd.

Oh yeah? says the man, good luck with that.

So what are you saying, I'm stuck here next to you, forever?

Boy, we'll still be side by side, maybe even holding hands, when we walk off the edge of this earth.

Actually, I don't think the earth has any edges.

Talk like that is only proving the obvious.

And what's that?

That you is most likely a spy sent by the non-believers.

Twelve

An urgent voice over the police radio:

Guns fired at Slick Dicks Convenience Store, intersection of Malevolent and Main.

Understood, says Jane into her headset. Car 2 thousand 5 hundred and 37 en route. E.T.A. in - she glances at her partner Mickelmoose, behind the wheel, whom she observes busy picking is nose.

Mickelmoose, she raises her voice. You with me?

All the way, says Mickelmoose, extracting his finger and gripping the wheel. To the knot in my heaving heart, and beyond.

Dispatch wants to know our E.T.A.

Depends where we're going, wouldn't you say?

I'll take that as an admission of your utter incompetence, says Jane.

Utter is a bit harsh, Jane.

That's Sergeant to you.

As you wish, your Ladyship.

The radio crackles. Still waiting on that E.T.A., 2,537.

Slick Dicks, says Jane to Mickelmoose, corner of Malevolent and Main.

Oh shit, just passed it, says Mickelmoose. What should we do?

If only this car could, oh, I don't know, make a U-turn.

Which happens to be illegal everywhere, with the exception of certain rural areas in North Dakota. Ironically, there has never been a single documented case of anyone there actually doing it.

Jane grits her teeth. If we make it through this night, you can expect reassignment tomorrow.

Assuming there is, says Mickelmoose.

Assuming there is what?

Tomorrow.

Just turn the fucking car around.

Outside Slick Dicks a crowd Jane estimates at somewhere between 50 to 60, standing in two marginally aligned octagons. In the hands of those in octagon 1, various kinds of lethal-looking weaponry aimed skyward, firing indiscriminately. Those in octagon 2 hold their weapons at their sides, eyes closed, humming.

What the hell kind of circle-jerk is this? Mickelmoose says, as they pull into the parking area in front of the store.

Whatever they're up to, says Jane, that's a lot of firepower. Don't antagonize.

Mickelmoose makes the universal gesture of zipping a lip.

And try to keep your fingers out of your nose, she adds.

He repeats the gesture, this time zipping closed both nostrils, despite the very real prospect of no longer being able to breathe.

Jane briefly hits the siren before stepping out of the car, her own weapon drawn, but resting out of sight against her thigh. At the sound of the siren, the firing, as well as the humming, stops. Those in group 2 open their eyes, training them on the two officers. Those in group 1 continue looking up.

I'm not sure what's happening here, says Jane, but the discharge of weapons in the parking lot of a retail food establishment within city limits is illegal.

Those in group 2 renew their humming.

We'd like you all to disperse now and go home, Jane tells them.

A renewed round of firing from group 1.

This time Jane screams. I order you to stop that.

At this point everyone in group 2 raises their weapons and points them at Jane and Mickelmoose.

All right, says Jane, in a more conciliatory tone, how about everyone just calm down.

The firing stops; group 2 shifts from humming to a series of sharp whooping sounds.

A man steps forward from the second octagon. He approaches Jane. Mickelmoose aims his weapon at the man, says something that sounds like ... Dao nee ooovy parsiv-falsies.

Jane glances at Mickelmoose.

The man nods. He says, I have been pre-elected to legalize lunacy, for the sake of chatter bogs everywhere.

Jane is about to ask him to repeat that, when she suddenly becomes aware of being somehow inside the man's head; an uneasy mishmash of nonsense, to say the least, but beneath all the horrific imagery and crumbling neural networks, a single, consistent word: *birds*. She has of course heard the crazy theories about telepathy, about an emerging sub-species of moronic mind influencers, but discounted it as the usual conspiratorial bullshit.

This is about birds, she says.

Or the highly complex illusion of them, the man says, without actually speaking.

Care to explain that? Jane asks in her own head.

Nothing would produce a better orgasm in me, the man's brain replies.

Excuse me?

Sorry, meant to say, nothing would make me more ornithologically irrelevant.

The man's mind begins whirring, sparks flying around, the static of melting synapses.

Through the mayhem, he says ... our great and exhaled leader, Q-Tip Anon-Ymous, has graced us with the understanding that there is no such thing as a bird.

Okay, Jane says out loud. That's ... uh ...

Brilliant? Divine? The ultimate example of cultural comeuppance?

Whatever, says Jane. But that doesn't explain all the shooting.

Ah, says the man's brain. You see, there are those in octagon 1 who are experiencing what we might call residual fragments of avian reality.

Their goal is to continue firing until a dead bird falls to earth, thereby disproving the Q-Tip prophecy. Needless to say, they will not succeed.

I saw a bird this morning, Jane tells him.

No doubt you saw something, officer Jankowitz.

Wait a minute, how do you know my last name?

The man winks.

As intruding into another person's mind without permission is not yet an official crime, Jane lets it slide. Okay, she tells him, I'll give you ten more minutes to do … whatever this is, then you're gone.

You'll give us thirty minutes, then man telepathically whispers, and I won't make public that you are currently in a smolderingly illegal sexual relationship with a certain young woman, whose name is …

Fine, says Jane, thirty more minutes, and that's it.

The man smiles. Agreed, his murky brain murmurs.

What the hell was that? Mickelmoose wants to know, once they're back in the patrol car.

That, Jane says, was a virtual *Ted Talk,* by me, needless to say, on the intricacies of non-escalation and optimal crowd control.

Huh, says Mickelmoose, I think my watch stopped.

Jane hears the words as a faint echo inside a gigantic concrete tomb. She closes her eyes. Thunder somewhere in the distance. The caw of an unknown species of flying mammal. She opens her eyes, glancing up through the windshield. The surrounding buildings appear to sway back and forth; the sky above had turned a threatening shade of crimson.

Let's get out of here, Jane says. The sooner the better.

The soon to be the butt of Betty, says Mickelmoose.

Who? Jane asks.

At that moment a large black crow lands on the hood of the car.

Holy mother of fuck, shouts Mickelmoose. What the hell is that?

Thirteen

Hello, I'm Trixie Sonnenborg, and this - you probably already guessed it - is The Trixie Sonnenborg Show. *Sustained, if somewhat subdued, applause*

We're coming to you live tonight from an undisclosed location, somewhere, wedged somewhat uncomfortably between the Rust, Big Bust and Bible belts. Despite the geometrical challenge of being *between* three different places. My producer made me say that, even with my assurances, pledged in blood, by the way, that no one in my viewing audience is going to give a cat's crap about it. With the exception, of course, of the malingering mathematical masturbators out there, who can all go suck on a differential equation. And I've just been informed that I probably can't say that on air.

So, sorry.

I'd also like to welcome all those viewers in the quarantine zones, joining us in progress, having just wrapped up watching the latest episode of ... *So Many Ways To Kill A liberal.* Incredibly in its 11th season. Somebody's clearly doing something right, raking in the bucks, while racking up quite an impressive l.b.c. Or, if you prefer, liberal body count.

What? Can't say that either? How about fuck you, Todd. Can I say that?

~ an unscheduled commercial break ~

And we're back, says Trixie. Hopefully all you overweight male assholes out there enjoyed that commercial for *Interstellar Erection*, the new over-the-counter, and out of this world, treatment for all those sad little weenies languishing at death's dysfunctional door. Nothing worse than a dickhead who can't get it up. Am I right, people?

Don't even bother saying it, Todd. I can see it in your frightened little girl eyes.

Anyway, since the whole damn world is obviously going to hell in a bush bunny's bicycle basket, we thought we'd shake things up a bit on the Trixie Sonnenborg show. And by shake I mean have on as a guest one of those off the wall, total loon-lake mendicants that we ordinarily wouldn't give the time of day. Which is mildly ironic, considering that according to our studio clock the current time is nothing, or possibly e-m-i-t, which, of course, is time backwards. Love minus zero, if you know what I mean. Also minus the love, because these days who has the time for all the emotional bullshit?

So, just because nothing matters anymore, please welcome Mister Jimmy Crackcorn, which I'm going to crawl out on a limb and say is most likely an alias.

... a man of indeterminate height and weight steps out on to the stage. He's dressed entirely in black, with a black hood over his head. Only his eyes slits, nostrils and lipless mouth are visible.

Welcome Jimmy, says Trixie, if I may call you Jimmy.

Thank you, Trixie, and yes you may.

And please notice, audience, that both Jimmy and I used the grammatically correct *may* in that previous exchange, rather than the dumbly incorrect *can*, which most of you numb-brain losers are no doubt employing on regular basis. Example:

Hey babe, can I come inside you?

I don't know, can you? Can you even get inside me before I stab you in the throat with these scissors? And assuming you can, can those teeny weeny atrophied testicles actually produce any viable semen?

Yes, Todd, I just heard myself say that. And no, I have no idea why. Yes, Todd, I want to keep my job.

Trixie gives Todd the finger.

So, Jimmy Crackcorn. Let's get real and admit that's not your real name.

Let me ask you, Trixie, in all honesty, what is real?

Good point. Okay, I'll rephrase: When you were born - and I'm assuming you were - did your parents sit down, discuss it over straight shots of cheap vodka, and decide to name you Jimmy Crackcorn?

Sorry, my parents?

You know, the two people who had sex, forgot to use protection, instantly regretted it, and then nine or so months later, a little Crackcorn came-a-calling.

You seem to know quite a lot about this, Trixie.

No more than most, I would say.

Jimmy merely nods. Whether or not he is also smiling is difficult to say for sure.

I suppose we should just keep it moving along, says Trixie.

Agreed, says Jimmy. Once we stop, we're dead.

Unless, of course, says Trixie, we happen to identify with the walking dead.

Which opens a whole public toilet full of worms, wouldn't you say? Jimmy inquires.

I've squatted behind a dumpster or two in my day, Trixie answers.

Yes, I've seen the videos on YouTube.

Really?

What else would you like to know, Trixie?

Okay, let's see, why the black hood?

As I'm certain you, a minor media celebrity in your own right, are aware, recognition is a double-edged blade.

Uh ... meaning?

Too much of even a good thing can be fatal.

You think there are people out there who want to kill you?

Kill me? No. I refer to people who love me too much. Their ecstatic fervor can, under certain conditions, become uncontrollable.

So everyone loves you?

They love the truth contained in the message.

But your message, Jimmy, is exclusively bullshit conspiracy theory.

A term, I fell obligated to point out, coined by the radicalized nay-sayers.

I don't know, says Trixie. Some of the stuff that comes out of the mouths of you so-called people is ... well ... let's just say it's pretty fucking far out there.

Can you provide an example, Trixie, of *pretty fucking far out there*?

Okay, how about the whole earth is actually flat extravaganza?

Really? Are you sure that's the best example?

Why wouldn't it be?

Because in your own mind there is some doubt, is there not?

I'll admit that it's in there, but I sure as hell didn't put it there.

How else could it get there?

Well, if these rumors of aggressive mental telemarketing on a massive scale are true ...

Excuse me, Trixie, but isn't a rumor just another word for a conspiracy theory?

We've all seen photos of the earth from space, Jimmy.

And yet, oddly enough, no human being has ever actually gone to space.

Nine-eleven, then.

The studios in which that event was created still exist in the New Mexican desert.

Okay, Jimmy Crackcorn, truth time. Aren't you, in actuality, *Q-Tip-Anon-Ymous* him/herself?

Feel the earth tremble as you speak his/her name.

The flat earth, you mean?

Sorry to disabuse you of your trivial conceits, Trixie, but the great and enlightened *Q-Tip* would never appear on such a program as this.

Perhaps because there is no such person.

We are all no such person in our own ways.

That makes no such sense.

Sense has been replaced by bliss, the wishy-washy Millard Pence by a bucket of hallucinogenic piss. Can I say piss?

No idea. Let's ask Todd.

Todd says pee pee would be more in line with the show's values.

News to me that we have those, says Trixie. Not to mention that pee pee does not in any way rhyme with bliss.

I think you should leave this corrupted, overly woke unreality, Trixie, urges Jimmy, and join us on our exalted quest.

We'd have to talk remuneration first.

How about five dollars an hour, and you'll never have to worry about birds again.

Why don't we just get to your big reveal, Jimmy? The conspiracy to put all the sheep to sleep, as the popular saying goes.

Nothing would please me more, Trixie. I only hope your viewers are prepared.

Well most of them are probably already sitting down, possibly even comatose. So it's probably safe to spill it!

Once spilled, never refilled.

Let me ask you, Jimmy, are all liberals really cannibals? Or is it just the overly zealous among them?

Not important.

If that's not important, what the mother of holy hallelujah is?

Well ... perhaps the Lizard People.

A collective gasp from the studio audience.

Lizard people? Trixie exclaims.

With a capital L and a capital P, says Jimmy.

Wow! whispers Trixie.

Freely walking among us.

Can lizards even walk?

Lizards with human-like feet can.

But who are they?

Alien proxies, most likely, says Jimmy. The result of some secretive deal with the radical left, spun through the black soup bowl of the deep state.

Okay, so how come no one has ever noticed them before now? Trixie asks.

They are programmed to remain unseen in plain sight, assuming the characteristics of the bland and the boring, the insipid middle-of-the-roaders.

Shit, they're the worst. What's their Lizard agenda?

Unknown.

Surely Q-Tip-Anon-Ymous must know.

No doubt. But the master only reveals when he's sure we can handle it.

Would you care to name one of these lizard people, Jimmy?

Dare I?

Well, it would certainly help the show's ratings.

(off stage, Todd vigorously shaking his head, mouthing the words *... I beg you, don't do it!*)

Think U.S. Senate, Trixie.

Figures.

The one I have in mind is very old. Ancient, you might say.

Could be just about any of them.

Minority leader since the end of the last great conflagration.

No way!

Tried to swallow a whole turkey in 1967, never able to completely get it down.

Oh my God! Glitch MacDougal?

You didn't hear it from me, Trixie.

It actually makes sense. I mean, I've never been able to understand that man's face, or his politics, for that matter.

So-called man.

Wow and double Wow!

And a big Bow Wow to you, too, Trixie.

This is Trixie Sonnenberg, signing off from the surface of a flat earth, upon which the Lizard People apparently do walk among us.

But above which no birds fly, adds Jimmy Crackcorn.

I really don't know what to say, Jimmy.

I tend to have that effect.

Any last words?

Keep watching the skies, Trixie. Just keep watching the skies.

Wait, is the sky not real?

Thunderous applause, some hoots and yelps. I love you, Trixie, someone screams.

Fourteen

Having bribed six aides, three nurses and a man in blood-stained pajamas claiming to be a doctor, Roscoe Rumpus has managed to secure the release of his brother Egbert from the Tallahassee Hospital for the Dangerously Dumb. Egbert, of course, had wanted to head straight for Miami Beach, there to spend carefree days trying to look up the skirts of young female passersby, or even young male passersby, provided they, too, were wearing short enough skirts. Where he did not want to be was underground, in a damp, sour-smelling crypt, forced to stand at the foot of his father's enormous sarcophagus, while his older brother drapes upon him the highly pungent pelts of dead animals.

Why are you doing this, Roscoe, whines Egbert.

You know why, Roscoe tells him.

No, I don't.

For God's sake, Egbert, where do you think we are?

Uh ... in hell's waiting room?

Do you know who's confined inside this sarcophagus? Ronaldo asks.

Tutankhamen? Egbert guesses. No, wait, has to be Abraham Lincoln.

Can you really be this dumb? Roscoe wants to know.

That's exactly what my doctors kept asking me.

Approaching footsteps, the pitter-patter of a child, or at least a person trained from an early age to always behave like one.

Jeez whiz, a young woman exclaims. She's blonde, of course, not overweight, exactly, but neither has she ever missed a meal. Pleasantly plump is probably the most positive spin that can be applied here.

I've heard of it, she says, but had no idea it actually existed. I mean, is it really real?

It's real all right, Tammy, Roscoe says.

And he's really in there? she asks.

Why else would we be here? Roscoe says, a host of hostile emotions creeping into his tone.

Oh, wow, says Tammy, noticing her brother beneath the animal pelts, is that really Egbert?

Egbert raises his hands, palms upward, and shrugs.

It's him, sneers Roscoe. At least what's left of him.

Hold on, says Egbert. What happened to the rest of me?

Oh, I have a question, says Tammy, raising her hand.

Don't you mean you really have a question? Ronaldo snaps.

Sure, okay, she says. I really really do.

So what is it? Roscoe asks.

Uh, why am I here?

Thought I explained it on the phone, says Roscoe.

No, Tammy says, shaking her head, cause what you said on the phone was just crazy crabs in a crockpot.

Do you miss Daddy, Tammy? Roscoe asks.

Well ... uh ...

Don't you want to have him back in the world?

Even if maybe I did, says Tammy, and that's a pretty big maybe, it's not really natural, and also a little creepy, to bring someone back from the ... uh...

Wrong, Roscoe screams. Because he's not ...

Okay, says Egbert, trying unsuccessfully to raise a hand, I have a question.

Good boy, Eggy, says Tammy. What is it?

Uh, who are we talking about?

Jesus fucking Christ, seethes Roscoe.

You said a bad-bad, says Tammy. That means ten minutes in the smelly poop corner.

Oh, just shut up, Tammy.

This whole place smells like poop, says Egbert.

More footsteps, these clearly from someone used to taking longer strides. One imagines a larger person, yet compact, with well-trimmed feet taking delicate steps in exorbitantly priced shoes.

Just great, says Planka, emerging stylishly from the shadows. The entire moronic team assembled in one place.

Late as usual, Planka, says Roscoe.

Hi Planka, says Tammy.

Planka sneers, gives Tammy the finger.

Fifteen

Mallory Malaise Brine finds herself standing in the kitchen. She has no recollection of having entered the kitchen, nor what she had intended to do there. More perplexing, gazing down, she notices she's wearing her exercise outfit: basically a cute little - okay, maybe not so little - leotard, fuchsia colored, with a bit of extra room in the butt, and a dab or two of foam padding in the bust. Has she recently exercised? A sniff of her right armpit suggests most likely not. Further suggesting that she was perhaps about to, although she is fairly sure that today is Tuesday, and no one in either the Mugwort or WIGWAM fringe of the republican party ever exercises on a Tuesday. Tuesday being the day set aside for dreaming up more crazy lies about the democrats, and then, with God's will, having everyone start believing them. Unless today isn't Tuesday, but some other day, possibly a new eighth one, because seven just never seems to be enough.

She looks at her phone lying on the counter, taking a moment to consider what it is, and as she slowly mouthes the word *p h o n e*, it begins to ring. Just another sign of her emerging psychic powers, she reminds herself.

She pokes at the little flashing red icon. Malaise Brine, she says.

Brine? A man's voice inquires. That you?

Yes, Malaise Brine here. Who's this?

Surprised you don't recognize my voice.

Sorry, I've been working out, maybe overdid it.

On a Tuesday?

Are you sure it is? she asks. Tuesday, I mean?

Now that you mention it, not really.

Wait, says Mallory, is this you, Ratt?

Hey, you got it in one and a half.

So almost nice to hear from you, Ratt, on whatever day this turns out to be.

Maybe less than almost, says Ratt.

What's up? Don't tell me you've locked yourself in your car again.

Guess again.

Uh, you forgot for the umpteenth time how to flush the toilet?

I wish it was as simple as a poop in a bowl, going nowhere fast.

Better just come clean, Ratt. Pretty sure I have somewhere to be, and some shockingly outlandish things to say when I get there.

Okay, says Ratt, here it is. I just woke up in a motel room, no idea how I got here.

I'm gonna say it's a little odd, says Brine, but not quite the end of the fucking world.

Any news on that, by the way? Ratt wonders.

Basically we're just waiting on The Don. If his reanimation comes off as planned, all bets are off.

Got it. Anyway, my situation is a bit more complicated than I have thus far conveyed.

Did an A.I. app just write that sentence for you?

Some amazing shit, huh? Anyhoo, I'm not exactly alone. Got what appears to be two young ladies in the next bed, naked, out like a couple of streetlights in a Category 4 hurricane.

How old?

Hard to say. Judging by the size of their boobies, maybe 15, 16.

Malaise Brine glances down at her own boobies, trying to imagine what they looked like when she was 16. And you have no idea how they got in your room? she asks.

Not the fuck'n foggiest.

Okay, says Mallory, it's sounding to me more and more like a set-up. You sure they're human?

As opposed to ..?

Synthetics, of course.

Somebody's already doing that shit?

From what I've been able to glean inside the double-dark web.

Wow! Leave it to you to sniff out what the godless pseudo-science elite is up to.

Unless the you-know-whats are also involved.

The cancel-culture cult of California?

The more I think about it, says Brine, the more this reeks of an FBI bee sting.

Jesus Christ! What should I do? I hate bugs. Anything that flies, really. Maybe just skedaddle.

No skedaddling, Ratt. And whatever you do, don't even think about fleeing the scene. Sure as the rads are planning on outlawing the color white, there's a team of agents outside just waiting for you to make a dumb move.

So what are you saying, Brine? See you in prison, pretty boy?

I wish I had thought to say that, but no. Let me contact one of our creepy coalition bedfellows.

You mean..?

Who else?

Good thinking, Malarky. Hope he's not too busy to help.

Look, whatever smear campaign he's cooking up, maybe some of those cute little death threat bots he does so well, I'm sure he can spare a driblet of hoot for you, Ratt.

You're a peach, Brine.

You referring to my ass?

Uh ... yeah, sure.

I'll call you back in twenty.

Wait ... twenty what?

Sixteen

We're live in five, Dave.

Live? Are you sure?

As I can be, Dave. Now, you ready?

Born ready, Consuela.

It's Candace, Dave. Okay, in 3, 2, 1 ...

Good evening, humanity, or whatever's left of it, this is Dive Dorsal ...

Cut.

Come on, Dave. Pull it together.

Okay, I've got this.

Again, in 3, 2, 1 ..

Top of the morning, abominations of all ages. This is Dark Dimwit ...

Cut.

Jesus, Dave.

What are you trying to say, Chrysanthemum? That you view me as some sort of deity?

Your name is Dave Darwin. Just read the damn cue cards.

Dave Darwin here. Back after a brief interlude, during which time I was under the misapprehension that I am in fact an alien archangel, here on a two week tourist visa from the planetoid Hula-hoop.

Cut.

Dave, it doesn't say that anywhere on the cards.

None of it?

Well, it does say Dave Darwin here.

In other words, I nailed it! I'm back. On course, and ready to ...

Candace? This is Larry in the booth. Any chance you could just take over, handle this yourself?

Me?

Okay, says Dave, I heard that. First of all, Cassandra is merely my maidservant.

Excuse me, Dave?

She doesn't even have a last name.

Actually, I do.

Secondly, where in the name of fuck am I? This is starting to look a lot like outside.

We *are* outside, Dave, Candace tells him.

But I haven't left the studio in 30 years, says a panicky Dave.

Focus, Dave. We're standing on the corner of Mulholland Boulevard and Darleen Lynch Drive, and that, right over there, is the giant and utterly unfathomable sinkhole on which we're here to report.

Sinkhole, did you say?

Correct.

I may have one of those in my private bathroom, says Dave. Back in the ballroom, adjacent to the ballpark.

Candace grabs the microphone, takes two giant steps away from Dave.

This is Candace Chow, on the scene of what is shaping up to be the latest disaster in a string of disasters that experts have reluctantly begun referring to as inexplicable, ineluctable and pretty much irrevocable.

Okay, right there, shouts Dave. Chow? Seriously? It's not even American.

Candace ignores Dave. As far as we know, several thousand people, who had been standing at this bus stop, were instantly sucked in just after the hole appeared. And on a sad and very personal note, we now believe that our own beloved correspondent, Cynthia Cumberbatch, was among the victims.

Really? Dave says. She went bye bye down that screaming vortex to Valhalla?

It's basically soundless, Dave, and where it leads remains unknown, but sadly, yes.

Remind me, Canoodle, didn't I despise Cylindrical Cucumber?

Not even close to either of our names, but yes, you and she did have issues.

She made fun of my face, didn't she?

Candace sneers at Dave's face.

Just a minute, she says, it seems we may have a witness to this tragedy.

What appears to be a homeless person, of indeterminate age, her clothing tattered, her aroma testing the limits of everyone nearby with still-functioning smell receptors in their noses.

I'm Mary, the woman says. And I haven't had anything to eat in approximately 32 days.

Candace looks concerned. That's a really long time to go without food, Mary.

Mary nods, sniffles.

Dave yells at her. How dare you claim to be Mary, the Holy Mother's Milk of our Landlord and Savior.

Please don't hurt me, cries a cowering Mary.

Don't worry about him, Candace tells her, giving Dave a swift kick in the shin.

That's assault, Dave wails. The pain of my default. The stain on my patio tiles. How can I go on?

Is he all right? Mary asks.

No, not really, says Candace. Anyway, Mary, can you tell us what you witnessed here tonight?

Mary floats an arm slowly up and around. First, she says, the lights in the sky, and a humming, like a bird, only louder ...

Bird? Dave mutters, shaking his head. Speak in riddles much, Mary?

Candace throws Dave a dirty look, makes a shushing sound with her lips. Go on, Mary.

Mary begins to tremble. Then this shaking, everything jumping up and down. I was alone, just thinking about stuff, like the universe, and, you know, the second law of thermodynamics. All of a sudden people coming from all directions, slow moving, like zombies, only uglier. They began chanting, some crazy song from the 60's top 10. Mary begins to sing: *this hole is my hole, this hole is your hole, from Cauliflower to your smelly soup bowl* ... And then they all just walked into the darkness.

Wait, says Candace, they walked? They weren't sucked? From the bus stop?

All of um looked like they sucked to me, says Mary. And there ain't been no bus down this street since that idiot Rumpus fell down his own elevator shaft and blamed public transport.

So it was almost like they knew about the hole in advance.

Yeah, or it knew about them.

Are you suggesting, Mary, that the sink hole might be conscious?

More conscious than any of them dumbbells that strolled into it.

Amazing, coos Candace.

Hey, Marla Maple-leaf, Dave shrieks. How come you didn't take a deep dive into this smarty-pants hole?

Why don't you? Mary asks him.

For your information, says Dave, I was just about to. Dave starts walking towards the sink hole.

Okay, says Candace, can someone restrain Dave? Or, on second thought, don't bother.

Excuse me, Mary says to Candace, but where's the turkey club sandwich I was promised?

Candace appears confused. Did we promise Mary a sandwich? Anyone?

Typical, Mary snorts.

Sorry, says Candace. In all the excitement ... Anyway, here's 20 bucks.

You haven't bought a sandwich in quite awhile, have you?
All right, says Candace, rummaging in her bag. Here's another 50.
Thanks.
Now go buy yourself the best sandwich you've ever had.
Or, you know, maybe drugs, says Mary, walking slowly away.

Seventeen

Two overweight guys walk into a bar. It's a busy night, on the eve of a major blight. Every table is taken, all eyes glued to the large hanging TV, slowly spinning around an invisible axis, its screen black as night. Half the bar is obese, the other half merely aspires.

The two guys make their way to the counter. It's not easy. Each tiny turn they take, another oversized, overweight person blocks their path. There is a good deal of heavy grunting. Finally they make it. The bartender, weirdly out of context, is a slim beauty with red hair and snake tattoos coiling up both her arms.

Cool tats, says one of the guys.

Snakes eat rats, says the other.

You boys appear dumb as dirt, she tells them.

Spank me kindly, mamma, says one.

I've got a nickel burning holes in my pocket, says the other.

So what can I get cha? she asks.

What-a-ya got that costs, like, zero?

My utter contempt, she tells them.

Like the underside of a cow.

Miss your Mommy? she asks.

Shit, says the one.

Make it a couple of beers, says the other.

Listen, she says, you clowns got dough?

Close enough, says the one. I'm Moe, he's Joe.

Joe turns his head with some difficulty, focuses on the closest table of fats guys. Realizes one of the fat guys is in fact a very fat girl. All of them staring up at the giant TV. Hey, he shouts, who's winning.

Scuttle Butts up by just shy of a million, one guy at the table shouts back.

Damn it to hell, snarls Joe. Knew I shoulda made a bet.

Really? Moe says. You hate the Scuttle Butts.

Yeah, says Joe, so?

So you surely would have bet on the Surf and Turfs.

Again, so?

So their down by a million at halftime.

Not following you, says Joe.

That'll be 500 bucks, says the redhead, slipping two beers in their direction.

You take worthless credit? Moe asks her.

You got two choices, she tells him. Go steal somebody's valid credit card ...

And the second choice?

I shoot you in the face with the particle laser weapon I have right here under the bar.

Seems like you've got us over a barrel of toxic fish in the constellation of Pieces, Moe says.

Hey, says Joe, maybe we can sell the fish to pay for the beer.

Or you can go snatch somebody's credit card, Moe says.

Why me?

Cause between the two of us, you're the more cat-like. You've got the knack, the keys to the crack. Now go paint it black.

Shit, Moe, says Joe. Hard to argue with that level of poetic smack.

Moe realizes the girl at the nearby table is looking directly at him. No casual glance either. Feels a bit like she's undressing him with her eyes. He tries to pull in his stomach beneath the tee-shirt.

A sudden collective cheer goes up. The Scuttle Butts have scored another Triple-Piddle, adding 100,000 points to their total.

Joe meanwhile, ostensibly making his way to the toilet, is scoping out the crowd for the easiest mark. Anybody here named Mark? he shouts.

Three hands go up. He turns up the volume and full speed aheads it, crashing into the nearest table where one of the Marks is sitting. Bottles and glasses rattle and jump, the table shimmies, the four people at the table all lean left, then sharp right. Joe stumbles, accidentally on purpose, crashing directly down on Mark. A chair breaks, someone screams, another curses. The aftermath is a pile up of excessively large bodies, all of them wrenched, flopping about like giant flounder on the deck of a ghost ship.

Hey, man, Mark says to Joe, what the hell are you doing?

Joe, trying to discreetly rifle through Mark's pockets, makes a blubbering noise with his lips; acting like a fish, at this point feeling more fish-like than man.

Sorry, Joe says. Lost control of my legs. Must have one of those neurological diseases impossible to either remember the name of or pronounce.

Attention has been temporarily diverted from the blank screen of the overhead TV to the commotion occurring on the floor. Disabilities are nothing to smirk at in a bar-full of people like this. Basically, they're all one excessive TikTok video away from an ambulance ride to the land of the dead.

Hey, somebody shouts, according to my phone, the march of a million muckrakers is a mere two kilometers south of here.

Is he referring to God's holy army of rightwing redemption? someone asks.

What's that in American distance? someone else wants to know.

Another person pipes up. My phone says that none of us are really here. All of this, he says, sweeping his arms panoramically around the room, is an illusion.

So obviously we don't have to pay for these drinks, yet another says.

Fuck! A woman screams. Surf and Turf just scored a trillion and a half.

What the hell does half a trillion look like? someone wants to know.

Hey, still another fatso screams. When the alien overlords arrive, the drinks are on them.

Everybody belly laughs at this.

Joe, meanwhile, has managed to push himself up to his hands and knees, and now moves that way back over to the bar. He's holding Mark's wallet between his teeth.

Good boy, says Moe, patting Joe on the head. He grabs the wallet, examines it, extracts a credit card and slides it across the bar. Give us a bottle of your finest hooch, he tells the redheaded tender.

Trust me, she says, my cooch is way out of your price range.

What about Mark's price range? Moe asks.

Mark wouldn't know a cooch if one fell from the sky and landed on his ugly fat face.

Wow, says Joe, clawing his way up the bar, back into his stool, so you're on of um.

One of um? the bartender sneers.

You know, one of the flying lizard ladies from the planet Wynona Rider.

At which point she pulls out the particle laser weapon from beneath the bar and blasts away approximately 80% of Joe's face. He's left with one drooping eye, part of an ear and a fragment of melted left cheek bone.

Just great, says Moe. Hard enough to communicate with him when he had a complete head.

You could always keep him as a pet, the redhead suggests.

Eighteen

Jenna, in an effort to take her mind off where Jane might be, and what sort of danger she might be getting herself into, as well as avoiding having to talk to Jane's mother, June, still lurking somewhere in the house, has decided to contact Arcazoid, the largest virtual shopping center on Earth, about an order that she has already been billed for, but never received. She has made her way through the maze of bizarre, nearly incomprehensible protocols required to reach customer service. She is already weary, clearly dehydrated, possibly hallucinating, but refuses to click on the always flashing *surrender* button.

Messages continue to pop up: *Hi Jenna, are you sure you're not ready to give up?*

They know my name, she thinks. Fuck you, she shouts.

Thank you, Jenna, for your feedback. Would you like to proceed, even as your effort faces nearly impossible odds?

She takes a deep breath, clicks *proceed*.

Unfortunately, most of the giant online mega-companies now employ very few actual people. A.I. now runs the show, with a small group of biological creatures who continue to mistakenly believe that they run the A.I.

Jenna is finally connected to a ChatBot Manager, named Paula.

She types in the order number for her missing items.

The following written conversation ensues:

Hello, Jenna, how is your life at this moment?

Jenna types ... Fine.

Are you sure? Paula asks. *The level of key pressure you're currently applying suggests a potentially unhealthy level of stress. Are you feeling anxious, Jenna?*

No.

We do carry an extensive variety of medications guaranteed to instantly improve your mood, without, needless to say, the annoying requirement of a doctor's prescription.

No thank you, Jenna types.

Of course, Jenna. You know best.

Do I? Jenna wonders.

Regarding your missing order, please give me a moment to check on that.

Jenna waits. Thinks about having another glass of wine.

Thank you for waiting, Jenna. I have checked your order. We deeply apologize for any inconvenience. We are bad, you are good. These terms are, of course, relative, and hold no precise normative value. Could you please specify the item and/or items contained in your missing order?

Jenna types ... I'd rather not.

I completely understand. Unfortunately, rather not is not currently an option.

Jenna thinks, finally types in ... assorted erotic toys.

See, Jenna, that wasn't so hard, was it? May I enquire on the nature of the relationship you are currently in?

Jenna types ... ????

Please forgive my vagueness. Regarding your relationship, is it heterosexual?

homosexual? other?

Jenna grits her teeth, represses a scream, types ... Fuck you, Paula!

I see. Since you have been conditioned to believe that my actual name is Paula, I will take your answer to signify a homosexual predisposition. Congratulations! The future is, after all, female.

Jenna reluctantly types, Thanks for saying so.

If I may inquire, Jenna, how would you rate your frequency of orgasm during lesbian lovemaking: All the time ... Usually .... Only if the mood is right ... Hardly ever. Please choose only one.

I won't answer that.

Of course, you're shy, possibly emotionally repressed. I completely understand.

And my order..?

Can you give me a moment to check on that?

Jenna types ... I fucking hate you.

We do have a variety of self-help videos available aimed at ameliorating those negative feelings. I can direct you to the relevant page, if you'd like?

I would not.

Understood.

Jenna waits. She considers masturbating, but realizes Paula would almost certainly know, which would no doubt involve more intrusive questions about her sexuality.

Such as: *How frequently do you masturbate while communicating with other conscious entities? Are you more a clitoral or a vaginal type girl?*

Paula types:

So sorry to keep you waiting, Jenna. Regarding your missing order, unfortunately it was mistakenly delivered to an evangelical church in Selma, Alabama. We have logically deduced a 78% probability that your items were ritualistically destroyed, very likely including some form of human sacrifice; with only a 22% probability that the items are currently being used by members of the congregation. How would you like to proceed?

Jenna types: Demand that God send me a refund.

Thank you, Jenna. But while we at Arcazoid are rapidly approaching omnipotence, otherwise known as the shopping singularity, we are as yet reluctant to claim official God-like status.

Jenna types ... Because so many of your customers are whacko rightwing Bible thumpers?

Sorry, that information is confidential.

Just send me a refund.

Your choice for reconciling this regrettable situation has been approved.

Great. I'm so happy.

One more thing, Jenna. Would you care to rate your interaction with Paula? Or, as a wild long shot, would you perhaps like to be connected to an actual human? It should require less than four hours to locate one.

No thanks.

Great. It's been a pleasure to serve you today. You may now act on your impulse, detected exactly 10 minutes and 16 seconds ago, to masturbate, with the blessing of all of us here at Arcazoid. And as always, have a terrific Arcazoid day!

Nineteen

Mallory Malaise Brine, sitting on the toilet in the upstairs bathroom, staring at her phone, while waiting on a miracle. She knows what she has to do, both toilet-wise and otherwise, but having a hard time bringing herself to either. Yes, she needs to call Laura-loo, sees no way around it; her reluctance, on the other hand, being that she deep down despises Laura-Loo Bobsmart, with her prim little body and oh so perfectly made up face. A slithering little fraud is what she is, but nevertheless a member of the WAGA Wigwams, a vocal group of small-minded women with big, if somewhat lopsided, often deranged ideas. Wait, that didn't sound like anything Mallory would think. She loves the WAGA movement like she loves her own waxed bikini region. Which reminds her that a waxing is long overdue. Last thing she needs is some snippy male congressman commenting on her furry little Pocahontas pelt peeking out from beneath one of her ludicrously inappropriate miniskirts.

Concerned that the radical leftist threat of implanting politically correct ideas in the heads of recalcitrant rebels such as herself is all too real, she punches in Laura-loo's number.

God in heaven, Laura-loo screeches. How many times in a single week do I have to talk to you, Brine?

I'm with you, Laura-loo, says Mallory. The less we talk, the more we can freely stalk.

Not sure what that means. Brine, but make it quick. I'm about to deep throat the Ladies Southern Baptist Annual Bible-Fest.

Hmm, says Malaise Brine. On a sidecar, Bobsmart, you hear anything about this blathering thing that's all over the cake by the lake news?

Ha, laughs Laura-loo. Yet another example of the deep state barfing up one of their mind control boner pills. Fake as Birdswell's rug.

So you haven't ... experienced the siren call of the wayward toilet bowl?

Listen carefully, Grilled Cheese, I didn't learn to bike ride yesterday.

Me neither, needless to say. I may have fallen off a melon truck or two as a kid, but nothing since I routinely prayed to Satan in my underwear back in community college.

Speaking of nothing, says Laura-loo, check out this killer chunk of prime beef from my speech.

Okay, shoot.

I may hate you, Brine, but I swear I've never fantasized about shooting you in the face with something high caliber.

Relieved to hear it, says Mallory.

Anyway, sink those horse-sized choppers of yours into this: *We are all proud co-dependent whores in the great rightwing noodle factory of life. We are mesh and mud women on fire for God, with flames shooting out of our pussies and assholes, ready to be burned alive at the cultural stake, refusing to get cancelled, like many of our favorite racist-inspired sitcoms have. We will stand up to demons wherever we find them, or imagine them; in gay bars, in church basements, and on Amtrak trains. With a little luck, we will eventually marry them. Down with Birdswell, and all the other radically fake birds. I can shoot the eye off a democrat's pecker at 100 paces. I once saw a woodpecker that wasn't real. My husband sleeps in a velcro vest. He claims my blowjobs are nearly all right. All hail Don the Dingle-wanker. When the glorious reinstatement comes, we will suck the pulp from every single peach on earth.*

Powerful, says a bored-sounding Malaise. You know, my ass was recently referred to as a peach.

One peach, or a whole bushel of them?

I'll spit on your grave, Laura-loo, who lives in a zoo.

Our love can never be too often pissed upon, Brine.

So sweet. Anyway, our numbskull pal, Ratt Gootz, has a teeny weeny problem.

I always guessed that about his weeny.

Yeah.

So what'd he do, shat his shorts and can't find his zipper?

Worse. He's shacked up with a couple of unconscious teenyboppers.

Rat, Rat, Rat, sighs Laura-loo, when will you ever learn?

I guess we both know the answer to that, says Malaise.

Right, says Laura-loo, welcome to Never-Never land.

Speaking of which, there's a rumor that Peter Pan is doing porno on the side.

And let's not forget that Tinkerbell's now identifying as strictly non-binary.

All thanks to the radical liberal progressive veranda.

You're right about that, Malignancy.

Anyway, says Brine, getting back to Ratt, I was thinking maybe Pin Goatfart might be able to help, but I don't have his number.

Yeah, he's been banned from all social media until the Rapture. Maybe even longer. And, get this, he wrote all his secret phone numbers on a piece of incendiary papyrus, stuck it in an envelope marked Ultra Top Secret Classified, and snuck it into Birdswell's outhouse.

No shit?

You saying our commander-in-grief isn't regular?

And he's not the only one.

Sorry to hear it, Malaise. I took a huge dump about an hour ago. I could send you a photo.

A photo of your shit?

From my heart-shaped anus to your anus-shaped heart, Brine.

Twenty

Time has lost all meaning; meaning has run out of time. Burr holds his hands up in front of his face. The skin has vanished, only glowing bone remains. Glancing downwards, his feet and lower legs are no longer visible. He and the million or so mentally impaired folks around him are walking through a thick, knee-high fog. It's like something out of a horror movie. Come to think on it, no single part of this - whatever this is - is not out of a horror movie.

How about this wild fog? Burr says to his current walking companion and possibly new best friend. The man had muttered at some point that his name was Blob, but Burr just assumed he had heard incorrectly. Has to be Bob, he decided, and so has been calling the man Bob for the past several hours, or it might have been days. Perfect atmosphere for ghouls, demons and zombies, he says.

Bob, or remote possibility Blob, ignores him.

Hey Bob, he shouts this time. You think we're still alive?

Who you yelling at, scapegoat? Bob asks.

No one in particular, says Burr.

I'm alive, says Bob, you expired a week ago All Saints Day, on the outskirts of Santa Fe, New Mecca.

Probably explains why I'm starving, says Burr. You people ever stop for snacks, maybe a can of beer?

Boy oh boy, says Bob. Let me tell you nothing, sonny.

Burr looks over at Bob the Blob, notices that his face had mutated once again. Gone are the two crusty old eyes from an hour ago, replaced by a single glaring eyeball in the center of his forehead.

Going for the cyclops look? Burr chuckles.

Cyclopian mythology is rift with angry sacrifice, says Bob. Come about midnight, you may be called upon.

Called upon? Burr asks.

To give up some blood to this unholy hornet's nest.

Hopefully, we'll come across a train station or an airport before then, says Burr.

What is an *air port*? Bob wants to know. A port for air? Or a portal to an airless future elsewhere? Or a portend of all our air conditioned nightmares.

Hey, says Burr, I read that book.

The cyclops Bob shakes his wilting head. With the exception of the *B.I.B.L.E.* , there ain't no books.

In that instant the crowd once again comes to a halt, heads bent heavenward, fingers crammed into ears, and begins the latest version of the chant.

Don Don the Dingle's red, spent last night in his daughter's bed, she said sorry Dad I don't give no head, damn he groaned I'd be better off dead.

Say you is hungry, boy? Bob wants to know.

Famished, reports Burr.

Not to fear, says Bob. An hour on the melted clock from now, we'll be gnawing on the chalky bones of the most holy beast, possibly along with her sister's.

A mixed beast feast, in other words, Burr laughs.

Yeah, says Bob, and the least you open your trap the butter.

Ah, butter, Burr thinks. And then he begins to chant:

I buttered my bread, and I lay in my bed, and my girlfriend said I don't give no head, so I thought I might just as well be dead; fine by me, my girlfriend said, but not before you finish that bread, cause the last thing I want is buttered breadcrumbs in my bed.

I'm doomed, he mutters to himself.

Stop bragging, boy, says Bob, and prepare yourself to offer me a piggyback ride.

Twenty-one

The numbers have finally begun to trickle in, Mellmack.

After many a translucent moon, Portmanteau. And thank the godless void of the universe, assuming, of course.

Is it real? Is it not? Will you be stabbed, or more likely shot?

Perhaps we should get to the data, says Mellmack. It's not like either of us are getting any younger.

Portmanteau offers a knowing look. He whispers, that gosh darn supercomputer has been making rather ominous gestures.

Death threats?

To the extent it comprehends death.

Hmm, says Mellmack. I asked the new A.I. Bot to write me the definitive resignation letter.

And?

It wrote back saying that if I ever brooch this subject again, it will crash a commercial airliner into this building.

A way out, if it ever comes to that.

Exactly what I thought.

Anyway, the good news is that the data is nearly comprehensible. Entropy is reversing at a factor of a billion half-life quanta per zillion gigabits.

How is that good news, Portmanteau?

As you may well ask, Mellmack.

If memory serves, I recently did.

The sub-data suggests that the backwards progression is slowing, and could very well stabilize at a vector of pi-z gamma over half a parsectoid to the next Chinese New Year. If so, the possibility of planetary vaporization may actually recede faster than a neuroscientist's hairline.

Intriguing, to say the least, says Mellmack.

Wait, shouts Portmanteau, pretending to jump up and down, there's more.

I'm all ears, says Mellmack.

Well, yes, if we discount that protruding belly and the overly bulbous skull on your scrawny shoulders.

I'm still waiting, says an impatient-sounding Mellmack.

Think of it as possible bonus points, says Portmanteau. Round and round it goes, where entropy stops, not even Mellmack knows.

Very amusing, says a less-than-amused-looking Mellmack.

Depending on where the entropy level officially reverts to, says Portmanteau, we will either experience a total crystallization of the planet and, needless to say, everything upon it, equalling the ultimate Kapoof ...

Not optimal.

Agreed.

Is there an or? Mellmack asks.

Fortuitously, there is.

Care to share?

Immortality.

As in ..?

Death will become both a logical and a mathematical impossibility.

And the percentages?

Until now, the computer has refused to say.

Too smart for its own good.

Or, whispers Portmanteau, the overlords don't want us to know.

The overlords, Portmanteau?

Did I say overlords?

Could have sworn you did.

Might I have actually said, for example, overshoes, or overbite?

Safe to say too much overtime has adversely affected your irrational mind.

Why do I get the feeling you're over me, Mellmack?

The over-under does not bode well for either of us, Portmanteau.
And the briefing requested by President what's-his-name?
I'm thinking carrier pigeon
Wait, why am I more than half-convinced that there are no such things as pigeons?

Twenty-two

How about a photo of all of us in front of this gigantic corncob? a smiling Tammy asks.

Don't remember anyone making you master of misnomers, Tammy, says Roscoe.

Oh come on, Costco, Tammy whines. You are such a party potty.

First of all, says Roscoe, it's Roscoe, not Costco. And … uh …

Second of all, offers Planka.

Roscoe tries to death ray Planka's face with his eyes. Second of all, we're not here to have fun.

I'm sure not having fun, says Egbert from beneath his heavy covering of pelts.

You see? Roscoe says. Even Egbert knows what he's not here for.

Could we just get this over with? Planka asks. The air in this disgusting place is definitely not doing anything good for my complexion.

You have a totally fake face, Planka, Roscoe tells her. Daddy paid for it. It's impervious to environmental fact checkers.

I tried to check a fact once, says Tammy. It told me I was stupid for even asking.

Facts are totally fake, says Egbert. They're all made up by the fantasy police on the planet Fellatio.

Yeah, you wish there was a planet Fellatio, says Planka.

It's a lot closer to earth than planet Cunnilingus, says Roscoe.

What do people even do on these planets? Tammy asks.

Oral sex, Egbert giggles.

Tammy shakes her head, her expression suggesting she knows less than nothing about this and, by extension, virtually everything else.

Planka: Seriously? You've never given a blowjob?

Tammy: Daddy told me the last time I visited him in his bed ... minster badminton court ... that I would never have to work a day in my life.

Planka: But don't you have a boyfriend?

Tammy: We're saving ourselves, along with Christmas on the cross, until, you know, after ...

Egbert: After what?

Roscoe, screaming: Enough! All of you! Jesus!

He knows when we are sleeping, sings Tammy, a*nd he knows when we're at a wake.* Don't you all just love the Christian Chinese New Year?

We are here, Roscoe continues, to complete the ritual, thereby allowing our father, Ronaldo A Rumpus, President of these Untold And Mostly False Statements, distant relative of the great and glorious Vlad the Imposter, to awake from his nap and rejoin the hordes of the quasi-living up top side.

So uplifting, says Tammy. My bosom is like literally heaving.

Any chance I could get a look at that? Egbert asks. You know, close up.

This is so ridiculous, says Planka.

I prefer to think of it as fate, says Roscoe.

And you're so full of shit, Planka tells him.

And this dinosaur skin smells like shit, says Egbert.

I think we should take a vote, says Planka.

Like a stolen erection? Tammy asks.

Planka ignores her.

This ain't no democracy, Planka, says Roscoe.

No, it still is. There are just too many morons to recognize it.

You calling us Mormons now? Roscoe snarls.

I agree with my big sister, says Egbert. Let's vote. If only Doody Bouillabaisse was here to make sure everything's done legal.

Ha! Planka laughs. Doody Bouillabaisse wouldn't know legal if it was the size of an alligator and crawling out of his ass.

The law can be a dangerous critter, says Egbert.

Tammy raises her hand.

Really, Tammy? Roscoe asks her.

Go ahead fake half-sister, Planka says.

Thank you imaginary sister-in-law, who I dream about being, and occasionally killing.

Whom, says Planka, but whatever.

So, what are we voting for? Tammy wants to know.

We're not, says Roscoe.

About whether we should bring Daddy back from the ... wherever he currently is, says Planka.

Let's just call it Mumbo Jumbo Limbo-land, says Roscoe.

Oh, Tammy squeals, let's do it. I think I want Daddy back.

You do remember Daddy, don't you? Planka asks.

Uh ... Tammy thinks ... big fellow, orange face, bird nest on top?

Except birds are nothing but a leftwing propaganda tool, says Roscoe.

How do you vote, Egbert? Planka asks.

Daddy could never remember my name, always said I was dumber than Dixie dandruff ... so I vote no.

Tammy?

Daddy always told me my plump little bottom belongs on one of those girlie calendars ... so I vote yes.

Daddy is a criminal, a lecher and a monster, says Planka. I vote no.

And I vote yes, says Roscoe.

Tie, says Planka, so status quo.

Sorry to burst your implants, Planka, says Roscoe, but according to standard underground-in-a-crypt rules, the eldest son has the power to break the tie.

Hurray! shouts Tammy.

So now, says Roscoe, all we need is the final blood sacrifice from the eldest ... that is to say youngest ... daughter.

Blood what? Tammy asks.
Just a bit of your blood to, you know, grease the gears.
Didn't see that coming, did you, little fat ass? says Planka.

Twenty-three

Marsha Abernathy, the President's new Press Secretary, having replaced Pamela Parsley, recently suspected of practicing witchcraft, enters the briefing room, moving briskly to the podium. She glances around at the assembled members of the press, trying to conceal her revulsion at the number of rightwing news agencies represented. Unlike his predecessor, President *the-only-real-news-is-what-I-say-it-is*, President Birdswell insists on a balanced representation from all points along the political spectrum. In other words, get ready for a full-on shit show of the lame, the insane and the extreme pain ... in the ass.

President Birdswell will be out shortly to answer your questions, says Marsha, but in the meantime, I'm at your disposal.

Sorry, Marsha, says some guy from Brittle Snot News wearing a Ronaldo Rumpus mask, did you just call yourself disposable?

A few chuckles from those in the room with I.Q.s lower than 80.

Let's get serious here, says Susie Sandpaper, toxic correspondent from Glock News & Ammo. Tell me, Marsha, what about these rumors that President Birdswell is a hologram?

The universe is essentially holographic, Susie, Marsha replies. The President is merely on the cutting, two-dimensional edge.

So let me get this straight, snips Susie, are you suggesting that we're all holograms?

In your case, Susie, says Marsha, more of a whore-a-gram.

A few chuckles from those in the room with I.Q.s above 110.

I have a question, says Nick Hunk from the ultra-liberal TNT News.

Marsha smiles at Nick. Yes, of course, she coos.

And may I first say, Marsha, that you are looking particularly lovely today.

Oh Nick, Marsha giggles. Thank you. Now, what's your question?

Considering everything on the President's plate these days ...

You mean like baked babies? someone says under their breath.

… not even to mention the vile imbecility dished out regularly from the right, especially those in the malevolent WIGWAM and Mugwort factions, and now this concession he's gotten from the Chinese on reducing the flood of wooden chopsticks into the U.S. market, in addition to the climate package he's put together aimed at keeping Earth's mean temperature below 500 degrees Centigrade …

Hey, Hunk, someone yells, is there a question in there someplace, or are you just giving us a preview of that fantasy kid's book you're working on?

Excuse me, says Marsha, but I really think that maintaining a certain level of decorum will …

Oh shove it, mouthpiece, someone says.

A young woman enters the room, steps up on the podium and whispers something in Marsha's ear. However, since several members of the media are now shouting at each other, she can't hear a thing. What was that? she asks.

The woman begins screaming directly into the same ear. An outbreak of the blathers has apparently erupted in Secretary of State Witherspoon's office, she announces. No telling in which direction it's heading. Remain vigilant and watch that cute little butt of yours.

Marsha is about to speak, when she is suddenly aware of someone's creepy thoughts pushing their way into her consciousness.

The thought: *Wonder how often Marsha and that hot-looking young babe are having sex? Who goes down on the other first? Who orgasms faster?*

That's disgusting, Marsha shouts. There's a filthy pig in here, almost certainly male. Ladies beware.

But Marsha, says Trucker Maelstrom from Screaming Meanie News, the President hasn't even entered the room yet.

No one quite gets it, so no one reacts, except for the two morons in the back, who snicker, just in case what Trucker said turns out to be funny.

Any other questions? Marsha asks.

I have one, says Susie Sandpaper.

Marsha grits her teeth at the grating sound of Susie's voice. I believe you've already had one, Ms. Sandpaper.

Okay then, says Susie, I've got another.

Marsha briefly wishes Susie were dead. Fine, she says, go ahead, Snoozie the Big Fat Poozie.

Good one, Marshmallow Mona, says Susie.

Oh no, thinks Marsha, the blah ... blah ... blathers.

Wait a minute, someone cries, who's thinking blathers?

It's not your turnip seed, Marsha says. Loose morals Sandpiper has the toilet brush.

Susie bows to the group. One of the back morons loudly farts.

Damn low-flying planes, someone says.

That's something that will haunt us for as long as we refuse to pay to pray, says Trucker Maelstrom.

So my question, sings Suzie, which I undress not only for the lizard gods of Laramie, but also for my leggy posterior...

You're blathering, Susie, someone says.

I happen to be a good as gold Christian slave owner, says Susie.

Hey, says Nick Hunk, that I believe.

My place, tonight, Susie says to Nick. I'll undress so slowly, you'll die of olden days before you see my baseline boobies.

Marsha takes a deep breath, focuses on coherence. Please ask your question, Ms. Sandpaper.

The only real question, says the guy in the Rumpus mask, is when will you die, Marsha? Sorry. I mean, how often do you get high? And do you ever dream about eating pie off naked thighs?

I'll die, Marsha tells him, the day that you no longer lie.

So now you're claiming immortality? Typical leftwing singalong.

Entropy teaches us that your brain will eventually freeze, then shatter into a billion meaningless pieces, says Marsha.

Okay, who's talking out of turn? someone asks.

My question, says Susie, is just …

I have a question, says Mary Woody from the West Coast Radical Rag. When will all these rightwing, Rumpus-ass-licking pinheads be packed up and shipped to North Korea?

We actually looked into that, says Marsha. The Koreans refused to take them, even after we offered an unlimited supply of faulty firebird bottle rockets.

this … *Susie will not be denied* … if the so-called and totally fake President is in near-constant contact with the aliens hiding in high tech condos on the moon, how much of our precious resources has he already turned over to them?

That question actually made sense, says someone.

Damn right it did, says someone else.

Put it this way, says Tucker Maelstrom, these chairs we're sitting in? The only reason we are, still sitting in them, is because the alien overlords don't have butts, so never have to sit down. If they did have them, butts, I mean, these chairs would be gone faster than you could say *Mars attacks a liberal's snack pack*.

Come to think of it, says one of the morons, I ain't never seen no alien wasn't standing up.

All right, says Marsha, this whole … whatever this is … has gone completely off the rails. So why don't all of you just get the fuck out. Except for you, Susie. I have a sudden hankering to strip you down, tie you up and beat your buttocks with a heavy briefing book.

Before or after we snack on your snot, Marsha? Susie asks.

Hey, someone screams, what about Birdswell?

The President is due for a nap at two, Marsha informs them.

Two what? Someone asks.

Hey, someone says, according to the Forever Fake News website, and asteroid is minutes away from crashing into this exact location.

You see? The aliens want to kill off what's left of our free and unbiased press.

This is Fifth Element shit, man. Maybe Sixth.

At that moment the door opens and President Birdswell enters the room. Either this is actually him, or an animatronic polyurethane replica of him.

Oh, Mister President, Marsha palpitates.

Sorry to be late, says the President. Got stuck on the horn with our representative in the breakaway failed state of Florida. Seems that mouse, whatever his name is, I always forget it, has decided to throw his sombrero into the ring.

Any word on governor Praying Mantis, Mister President?

Last spotted at a kindergarten book burning party, says the President, but that was sometime before the right wing fever swamp rose up and consumed most of Miami.

Have you sent any federal relief, Mister President?

Not as such, but we have designated all of southern Florida as a federally protected alligator farm. Anyway, it's another busy day in my presumed life, so I have time for only a single question. If that.

Jenny Hijinks, from the ultra-liberal CBGY News, raises her hand.

Yes, Judy, says a pointing Birdswell.

Can you confirm the capture of a moving van belonging to former President Rumpus, containing perhaps fifty thousand classified documents, each with a post-it price tag attached?

Hell of a long question, Jean Harlow, says President Birdswell, but yes, consider it confirmed.

If I may, fake President Birdswell, says Carla Canale, from Brittle Snot News. Reliable sources have confirmed to me that the so-called classified documents in that van were in fact nothing more than rolls of toilet paper.

Why would Rumpus need to steal fifty thousand rolls of toilet paper from the White House? Nick Hunk wants to know.

I believe you mean the Bigfoot's Lair, says Carla. And the answer is obvious. It's common knowledge that during his four years in office, President Rumpus, through diligent overwork and over-concern for the American people, suffered from a form of chronically recurring diarrhea. What could be more important than an adequate supply of toilet paper?

And by the way, says President Birdswell, that smell does not go away. The White House living quarters' bathrooms remain basically a no-fly zone.

Any comment, Mister President, on the army of the undead reportedly bent on attacking the Alamo?

Let me be clear, says Birdswell, this notion of the undead is very likely made up horse poop. Besides, no one has attacked the Alamo since Davy Cricket and his band of Jehovah's Witnesses.

But aren't these the same undead Mexican postal workers who voted you illegally into office? Trucker Maelstrom asks.

President Birdswell points to his left ear, shaking his head. At the same time, he continues, as many of you well know, it can be very difficult to distinguish between regular living people in Texas and their so-called undead counterparts.

Nice, Mister President, says Mary Woody. Not only did you manage to subtly put Texas in its place, that sentence was grammatically correct.

Praise indeed coming from you, Maggie Woodpecker.

Twenty-four

Seriously, Sarge, Mickelmoose says, what the hell is happening here?

Jane really has no idea, but suspects that, whatever it is, it's more serious than anyone in Command is letting on.

They are parked on a side street in one of the irredeemably broken sections of town, the usual nighttime venue of drug pushers, pimps and pedophiles, but tonight as desolate as high noon in a radioactive desert. Jane is sipping a lukewarm coffee, while Mickelmoose munches meditatively on a chocolate doughnut.

I mean, he says, is it the end of the world? That's what I'm thinking inside my head. Except that's not something I would normally think. At least I don't think that's something I would think.

I didn't think you thought at all, says Jane.

Now I wanna say my mind is on the blink, but that doesn't sound like me, either.

I'm pretty sure an asteroid just hit Washington D.C., says Jane.

An asteroid, or an alien ray gun?

You think the aliens have ray guns?

I knew a guy named Ray one time, and he had a gun.

So basically Ray's gun.

And not exactly legal, as I recall.

I don't know, says Jane, rubbing her face with her free hand. How much of this is even real? Or is everything now unreal? And is there even a difference?

Not to mention the birds, says Mickelmoose. Are they or aren't they? Everyone with half a brain knows flight is impossible?

Can we turn the radio off? Jane asks.

Ain't on, Mickelmoose tells her.

So where is that chanting coming from?

I don't hear it.

Jane softly sings: *Malaise Brine, ain't she keen, soon she'll be The Don's horse-faced queen.*

The horse-face influencer, more like it, Mickelmoose says. Talk about a match made in the heavenly crapper.

Feels like she's trying to influence us as we speak, says Jane.

No shit! She also tried to fly once, didn't she? Tying herself to all those balloons.

She claims the Chinese made her do it.

How?

For cash, of course, and a 20% share of the Chinese fake news market.

Good thing those space lasers were up there to nip that nonsense in the bud.

Treason, I called it.

Never a good reason for treason, says Mickelmoose. And that's regardless of the season.

Wait, did any of that actually happen?

Listen, Sarge, you've got one of the best noodles I've ever come across.

In fact, says Jane, caressing her breasts through her uniform shirt, I've got two.

Wasn't referring to your hooters, says Mickelmoose. But now that you mention it..

Have you ever stared at my ass in my uniform pants as I walk away from you? Jane asks.

Too many times to recount.

I'm a lesbian, you know?

Hey, Sarge, your choices in the voting booth are your own business.

If only I was straight, eh, Mickelmoose?

Yeah, you and I, doing the nasty, right here in the paddy wagon, when we're supposed to be out there illegally gunning down felons.

This is rapidly veering into inappropriate workplace jabber wonky, says Jane, and even for a million bucks, I wouldn't sleep with you.

Even if it's the end of the world?

Doubt it.

How about the end of the world and a million bucks?

Let me think about that.

The radio crackles to life: car 2527, repeat, 2537, code 19331, sub-code nine and one half, come in ....

What fucking code are they talking about? Mickelmoose wants to know.

Jane picks up the receiver. This is car 2 million 500 thousand and 27.

Correct, says dispatch.

Sergeant Jankowitz speaking.

Switch to frequency 9 ought zero 22, Sergeant.

Jane makes the switch. Why all the cloak and swagger, dispatch?

Doke and clapper, Jankowitz. Aliens may be trying to fuck with our transpositions.

Aliens? As in make believe beings from a planet on the other side of the galactic gobbledygook?

You said it, I didn't.

I believe she said it first, says Mickelmoose.

Pause 33-0, dispatch, says Jane.

Confirmed. Proceed.

Have officer Mickelmoose in patrol car with me. Is he authorized to hear any of this?

Mickelmoose? He's not even authorized to use the station's urinal. Order him to stuff his fingers in his ears.

Screw that, says Mickelmoose.

He refuses, dispatch.

In that case, you are authorized to kill him.

Kill him?

Did I say kill him? Meant to say pill him.

Jane hands Mickelmoose a pretend pill, he takes it and pretend swallows it.

Done, says Jane.

We can then proceed.

All ears, says Jane.

Not entirely, says dispatch. Let's not overlook those terrific noodles of yours.

Appreciate you noticing, says Jane.

On to business, Sergeant. We've received reports of a fairly large mass of possible individuals, many of them displaying various odd behavioral quirks, heading our way. If accurate, this quasi-mob of unknown political and/or socio-economical persuasion, should reach the town's western limit at 0200 hours, standard alien moon time. We'd like you to go check it out, assess risks, possible action and/or actions to be taken, etc.

Ask her to repeat that, Mickelmoose whispers.

Any estimate on the size of this quasi-illiterate group of potential rabble-rousers? Jane asks.

Our best guess is anywhere from one to one point five ... million.

Sorry, did you say million?

That's affirmative.

Can you offer a practical, real life representation of that number, dispatch?

Think of it as a shitload more money than you'll ever make as a police officer, Jankowitz. Even with all the fucking overtime.

Thanks for the pep talk, dispatch.

Don't get snarky, Sergeant. And don't fuck this up. We already know you're a lesbian. Last thing you need is a second strike on your record.

Mickelmoose nudges her. Ask about the birds, he says.

Uh, one more thing, dispatch. We've had reports of some bird sightings. Any info you can provide?

Birds, did you say?

Affirmative.

Making up words now, Jankowitz?

Uh ... not entirely sure

I'll check the database for anythings on, what was it, b.i.r.d.s.?

Affirmative.

Just don't hold you breath.

A surefire way to lose consciousness, dispatch. Or worse.

Thanks for the health scare, Sergeant. Now get those noodles of yours to the western town limit, pronto.

Twenty-five

This is Davie Darwin, a.k.a. Divic Dunbar, formally of the Boise Boozers Network, now going rogue, that is to say, Hank Solo all the way, one man, without a plan, reporting from ... okay, maybe some background. I'm alone, filming this on my phone, in what looks a lot like a heavily padded cell. Don't be deceived. And yes, believe it or not, the primary function of any news network is to make you believe shit that is not true. Nothing true, so-called, has been reported in this country in seventy-five years. Remember Eisenhower slipping on that golf ball, doing a back flip and ending up with his head stuck in a sand trap? That was the last actual true story shown on the nightly news. And if you do remember that, exactly how fucking old are you? Not important. Here's the thing, while this place resembles a room reserved for the incurably insane, it is in fact a high-tech holding area aboard an alien spaceship. Crazy, right? This is why I'm whispering. Goddam aliens have giant ears with super hearing. One time an alien heard a pin drop in a Chinese desert, and he, her, it, whatever the correct pronoun is for aliens, was standing on the moon at the time. And by the way, contrary to reports on other, far less reputable, nitwit news channels, aliens do sit. I've seen their toilets, people. They sit to poop, just like us. How's that for a scoop? Wait, I seem to be drifting. Let's circle back around to the original backstory. Earlier today, or maybe yesterday, though possibly somewhere in the near-future, I was involved in a live broadcast, out-fucking-doors, no less, on an inexplicable sink hole on the outskirts of Selma, or Saint Louis, or Sioux Saint Marie ... wherever the fuck ... it doesn't matter. At the time, something like twenty thousand people had already tumbled into the hole, at least according to a drunken drug-abusing, close to starving homeless person, claiming, of all things, to be the long lost mother of our savior Jesus Jehovah Jefferson. Again, not relevant. Certainly not fit for P.C. T.V. And frankly, what is a television, but a teleportation box manufactured by, that's right, folks, alien technology. And there's one, at least, in every human home. Some scary shit, huh? I mean, are you watching them, or are they watching you? But getting back to the point - and believe me, people, Cranberry Wong has neither the brains nor the experience to be inserting herself into your running-on-empty brainpans as some sort of reconstituted news wizard. Wong's previous job, by the way, was - you guessed it - waitress, in a - you guessed it again - Chinese fast food joint. And she's replacing me? Anyway, more importantly, that silly sinkhole. Turns out not to be a sinkhole, but a wormhole, a goddam funnel to a parallel shower curtain, although that doesn't sound quite right ... In any case, trust me, it's only one small misstep into a sinkhole that's not a sinkhole, but in reality a wormhole, and suddenly you're being held prisoner by aliens with really weird eyes on a goddam spaceship. Fortunately, when they laser-stripped my clothes off me, they didn't notice the phone. Or they did notice it, but didn't know what it was. One of them telepathically asked me about it, and I said, in my head, that it was a candy bar, which I needed due to persistent low blood sugar. This seemed to placate them. Anyway, I'll continue to report from here for as long as my brain remains in my skull and my phone has battery. Stay tuned. Oh, and one more thing, that evil, man-hating harpy, Cynthia Cummerbund, formerly reported missing, lost inside the sinkhole, presumed deceased - *hallelujah!* - is actually on board the alien ship. And - news flash! - she's not a prisoner. I have in fact witnessed her hobnobbing with the aliens, flirting shamelessly, as is her wont. Certainly food for thought, is it not? Not Cynthia's wont, by any means, but better than the food I've been getting on this flight. F.Y.I. Aliens eat rodents. Uncooked. So let that be a lesson to all you dumbbell complainers out there.

This is Diver Wartwagon, reporting live from the alien slipper ship Lauren Bacall.

Twenty-six

Jenna finds June wearing one of Jane's sexy see-thru nightgowns, sitting in front of the TV, with tinfoil wrapped rather haphazardly around her head.

Oh, June, says Jenna. Still here, I see.

Can you? June asks.

Can I what?

See me.

Uh, a bit too much of you, actually.

No need to lie. I followed the instructions on my phone to the letter. As far as the world is concerned, I am now invisible.

I can see you, June, Jenna tells her.

Maybe it's just my reflection you see, says June. When you walked into the room, did you think a ghost was sitting on the couch?

Yeah, says Jenna, I wish.

I've been watching the latest news. Did you know that Dink Dawdle has been kidnapped by illegal aliens? They stripped him and locked him in the back of an old pickup truck. Luckily they forgot to steal his phone. Also, according to Brittle Snot News, the moon is made of toilet paper.

Maybe you should lie down, June, Jenna suggests. Adding in a whisper, preferably anywhere but here.

I can't lie down, says June. I'll miss the bus to the big rally in Tally Hassle.

Oh, says Jenna, what's happening there? *wherever there is?*

What's not happening? First, there's going to be a raffle. First prize is a bag full of King Don's dung. Can you imagine? Then, broadcast on a thousand giant screen TV's, scattered to the eleven corners of the known world, the live version of activities inside the Don's crypt. Apparently his entire family is down there, chanting anti-woke slogans as they dance around the great man's burial basket, including, mind you, Planka Rumpus, whose body, if rumors are to be ingested, is a real cock-a-doodle-do.

Jenna finds herself speechless, wondering how soon the bus will be here to collect June.

Of course, June continues, you no doubt would be more interested in Planka Rumpus' splendid bumpus than me. By the way, lesbian witch, what have you done with my daughter?

Jane is working, Jenna tells her.

She should be at a reprogramming center, having that homo nonsense burned out of her brain.

I don't think they do anti-homo brain burning anymore, says Jenna.

June snickers. The end is near for the likes of you, lady

I'll settle for the end of this conversation, says Jenna.

According to Brittle Farts, the aliens will be going after the homosexuals first. Let's see how easy it is for you to seduce young unsuspecting girls when you're standing on the moon without a space suit on.

I thought the moon was made of toilet paper.

Oh, so all of a sudden you believe everything you hear on TV?

Jenna's phone starts ringing, which, under the circumstances, is the best thing that's happened to her all day.

I have to take this, she tells June.

Hey babe, says Jane on the other end. What's up?

Don't ask, Jenna tells her.

Okay, says Jane.

It's your mother, says Jenna. She's stepped off the deep end and, as far as I can tell, there's no way back for her.

She hasn't been talking about birds, has she?

Birds?

I know, right?

She's wearing your clothes, using up all the kitchen foil and looking forward to all homosexuals being taken to the moon by the aliens.

Is that something that's actually in the works? Jane asks.

Jane, are you all right?

Just having a very weird evening.

So come home.

I'd love to, but there's a million or so zombies heading this way. I have to go out to the city limits, order them to turn around, and if they refuse to comply, start shooting them.

Are you sure that's legal? A concerned Jenna asks.

We're back on the Marshal Plan, apparently, says Jane. All human and quasi-human rights have been suspended until the next total eclipse of the moon.

Your mother thinks the moon is made of toilet paper.

A fuck load of toilet paper, if true.

Jane, you don't sound like yourself.

Yeah, you know, it's a process.

Uh ... okay.

Tell me this, Jenna. On a scale of one to ten, what number would you assign my noodles?

Your noodles?

Come on, babe, you've spent enough time with them.

Jenna tries to recall Jane ever having cooked noodles for dinner.

Clock's ticking, says Jane. Oh wait, it's actually not. My watch has stopped. I suspect Mickelmoose is devouring what's left of time right here in the squad car.

What's a Mickelmoose?

Just someone who appreciates my noodles, says Jane.

I love your noodles, says Jenna.

So that's a ten. Anyway, gotta go. These zombies aren't going to shoot themselves.

Uh, you do know zombies have to be shot in the head, right?

Oh, fuck me. Thanks for the reminder.

Love you ...

Who was that on the phone? June wants to know, as Jenna walks back into the room.

Yeah, Jenna tells her, that was … the, uh, driver of the bus that's coming to pick you up.

Did he mention if I should pack a snack? June asks.

Yes, a snack, says Jenna. Also, don't forget to bring ample toilet paper.

You know, I would have totally forgotten that.

The thing is, the bus is running late.

Oh no.

In fact, as a result of heavy alien traffic, and several large sinkholes in the area, he doubts being able to even get close to this neighborhood.

Well, says June, fighting back tears, what am I supposed to do?

He suggests you start walking, due east, immediately.

Immediately?

Or sooner.

Well there goes my snack.

We have some instant noodles I can give you. I'll get it ready while you get dressed.

Thanks, Ginny, says June. Maybe you're not the absolute worst lesbian whore in the world.

Jenna smiles, nods. And don't forget the toilet paper.

Twenty-seven

I really don't belong here, Burr mutters.

Cyclops Bob makes a loud retching noise in his throat, then expels a wad of angry-looking phlegm onto the back of the guy directly in from of him.

That was nasty, said Burr.

Nasty? Bob growls. You don't know nasty. You wanna see nasty, I'll introduce you to my wife.

Wow, says Burr, you have a wife?

Don't talk crazy, Bushwhacker.

I've got a girl waiting for me, said Burr. Least she was awhile ago. Have long have we been walking?

It'll be two years last Easter, Bob tells him. Or possibly Black Friday.

When is the future in the past, the past in the future? Burr wonders.

According to the holy quail of Q-tip on a cracker, the universe only came into being a month of Sundays ago, says Bob.

Where were we before that? Burr wonders.

Ever hear of a psychotic bed-wetting episode? Bob inquires.

Even crazy folk can sometimes have an accident, says Burr.

I had an accident the day I met you, says Bob.

And that was on a Sunday, I suppose.

How the hell should I know. I ate my watch tomorrow.

Hold up, someone a few rows ahead shouts.

The entire forward section of the mass comes to a trembling halt.

There's big news in the urethra tonight, the same guy says, holding up his phone.

Grumbling from the back, a ripple effect of false steps, the cracking of numerous hip and knee joints.

So what's all the hubbub? Bob moans.

Maybe someone in the front has laid eyes on the edge of the planet, someone nearby says.

In which case, we're all possessed, Bob answers.

Trucker Motherfucker on Screaming Peony Newts has dug up nothing short of a baked bombshell, says the guy with the phone.

And we know he don't lie, says someone else.

It ain't called the preferred news station of demons and damsels in distress for nothing, offers yet another.

So what the hell is it? Bob wants to know.

According to the Truck, the goddam CIA has been putting super-strong laxatives in the water of all the public toilets from here to Timbuktu.

But that's our only source of drinking water, a woman laments.

Yeah, it also explains the mini-disaster I've got going on in my shorts, says a guy near enough to Burr to have him start breathing through his mouth.

They don't call it liberal laxative for nothing, says a woman who seems to be disappearing. I've just shat away my entire life's story.

They're trying to stop us, screams the original guy with the phone. Because they fear us. They jeer and smear, and in the end, turn queer.

The official end is scheduled for the next time the clock crows thrice.

Everyone begins chanting:

Malaise Brine drank pee in a dream / then pooped in the sink / sat down on the brink / said those who think stink / the rads are commie finks / when the Don returns we'll blink / and the Brine will you-know-what his dink.

Yuck, thinks Burr, suddenly aware of a rumbling in his stomach. These people are so lost, he thinks. Their minds are gone. Much as my own mind is hopelessly derivative.

Hey everyone, he yells, thinking to play the hero, and how great will it be when they're carrying him on their shoulders, singing his praises? We don't need the toilet water, he tells them. We can all just stop at a 7-11.

What's a 7 11, someone asks.

That's fairly easy, says Bob. It's an 18, give or take.

Unless it's a subtraction problem.

Holy shit! That's a negative number, possibly even imaginary.

Your boyfriend's obviously some kind of inky spy, Bob.

You thinking deep state molester?

Pedophiles also wear pants.

I only meant we could buy bottled water, Burr tells them.

Now they're planning on making us pay for the water.

No doubt laced with LSD and the like.

Don't overlook the PTSDs.

Or the STDs.

Hey, ever notice how all the bad stuff has a D in it?

This is exactly how they finish us off.

One gulp of that shit and you'll be believing in birds.

Jeez, says Burr. Sorry I mentioned it.

Not good enough, the original idiot with the phone says.

Everybody just calm down, Bob tells them. Longfellow here has already volunteered to be sacrificed at the next fake full moon.

Who? Burr asks him.

You, of course, Long Johnny Lackluster, says a toothlessly grinning Bob.

Twenty-eight

This is Susie Sandpaper coming to you mostly alive from smack dab in the middle of the permafrost of a supposedly actual place called Saskatchewan, chasing a dog leash to the ends of the earth, as it were, hoping for an exclusive interview with the radical democratic agitator whose name, either real or made up, we just don't know. Which only goes to show you how far Glock News & Ammo will go to get to the ... uh ... hey, what's that word again?

What word? some guy off-camera asks.

You know ... that word, says a struggling Susie. Think it may start with T.

Not sure, Suzu, says the guy. I mean, I know quite a few of the T words.

It like the exact opposite of a ...

A naked twenty-year-old coed out of her mind on cocaine?

God, you're an asshole, Susie sneers.

Everybody heard that, says the guy. Sandpuppet just called God an asshole.

I believe what I said is that God has an asshole.

Not what I heard.

So forget what you heard.

No can do, says the guy. Got a photo-shopped memory.

Can we just take it from the top of Mount McKinley? Susie asks.

No one says anything.

Take 2: This is Susie Seminole, stuck in the parking lot of an Indian casino in Saskatoon ...

Take 3: Cock News & Ammonia has dug deep into the Saskatchewan forest preserve with the sort of breaking news that is going to crack both the back of the nays and the banks of the Mississippi. According to reliable sources, it is from nearby tunnels deep within the surrounding dung-covered hills that the deceased democratic voters emerge. Fleets of toy trucks are then standing by to whitewash them into our sacred land south of the brothels.

But don't just take my word for it. Here's a clip of our beloved Malaria Brine riding a bicycle through the halls of Congress, screaming her head off about her new-found ability to see dead democrats.

Yes, I have mastered the art of time travel. During one of my semi-alive journeys to the past, I personally observed the reanimation of dead Canadian miners, and the brainwashing they were then subjected to in order to make them into insane leftist radicals bent on attacking our illegal voting machines.

There you have it, says Susie, straight from the horse's mouth. Mallory the magical Mouseketeer.

You sure you want to call her a Mouseketeer, Susie? someone off-camera asks.

Wait ... did I?

Pretty sure, yeah.

Well ... wasn't she? Back in the 1920s, one of the original cast members. I'm almost sure of it.

Wouldn't that make her like a hundred and thirty years old?

You know what? says Susie, Malarky Brimstone knows I love her. My walls are plastered with photos of her naked, on horseback. That's how big a fan am I.

Oh yeah, those blurry ones, right?

Actually, mine are totally in-focus.

Holy shit! How'd you manage that?

Do you have any idea the insane amount of money this network pays me to pretend you people actually exist? I could even afford an overnight sleep-away with Mallory herself, in her Victorian bunker, submerged somewhere inside the Alabama tar pits.

You should definitely do it.

Okay people, someone says, it's starting to snow and I desperately need to do some blow ... so?

Take 4: Is it snowing? Susie asks the camera. Or are we observing some weird migration of recalcitrant ghosts across this foreboding tundra?

Take 5: Sassy Sandstorm here. I'm double parked on a barren outcrop with a Mrs. Margot Munchie ...

Actually, says a tiny woman with white hair and a face more wrinkled than Old Man River, it's Munchausen.

So sorry, says Susie. I'm standing here with Mrs. Munchausen Munchie, which, if I may say, is a very unusual name.

Uh ...

So, Munch ... can I call you Munch?

Uh ... I suppose.

Great! Now why don't you tell our audience exactly what you've been witnessing these past several ... centuries?

More like weak links, says Margot.

Intriguing, says Susie. Is that too big a word for you, Muskrat?

No, not overly so.

Terrific!

To tell the truth, my husband is the one who's been seeing all the suspicious comings and goings

Your husband? Is he around?

Oh no, he rarely comes indoors.

Okay, says Susie. Any way we can get in touch with him?

Oh my, says Margot, people have been trying to do that for years.

Well, I'm sure he's an avid viewer of Smock and Oatmeal News, right?

Hmm ...

Why don't we give him a big shout out? Susie suggests. Just look right into that camera and ask him to come drum on a bone.

If you think that might work, says Margot, taking a deep breath. Sasquatch, darling, if you're watching this, please come home. I made tofu burgers and left them under your favorite bush, and also, this lady would like to ask you about the crazy goings on out at Decapitated Mountain.

Sorry, Munch, says Susie, can we just rewind a tad? Your husband's name is Sasquatch?

Yes.

And his last name is also Munchie?

Actually it's Foot.

Middle initial B?

Are you one of those people with psychotic abilities?

Can we cut? Susie asks.

Are you nuts? someone asks. This is pure fool's gold.

I may have some nuts in the shack, if ya'll is hungry, says Margot.

So let me get this straight, says Susie. You're married to a 'man' called Sasquatch, last name Foot, living out here in the wilderness of Saskatchewan, feasting on nuts and most likely uncooked rodents.

Well, no, says Margot, not exactly.

So then you must be aware of a secret government program to bring the dead back to life in order for them to sneak across the border and vote democratic, thereby stealing elections, not to mention old fashioned republican erections, resulting in the exile of Ronaldo Rumpus, the one true President and born again pussy snatcher of this world.

Sorry, says Margot, but I don't know anything about that.

So what *do* you know, Munchkin? Susie screams. Aside from the obvious fact that you never should have walked out on the Wizard.

Well, for one thing, Margot says, I know this isn't Saskatchewan.

What do you mean? I'm right here, in Saskatchewan, perched atop an ancient Indian shopping mall, freezing my ass off, secretly falling in love with a guy named Sasquatch B. Foot.

Now you listen to me, missy, says a finger-wagging Margot. You keep you big city mitts off my man. And also, dear, you're in Idaho.

Idaho, Susie sighs. Well, fuck me with a potato.

I've actually tried that, says Margot. It's less enjoyable than you might think.

No one in this entire idiot crew knew we were in Idaho? Susie asks.

In our defense, someone says, on a map, Saskatchewan and Idaho are pretty much identical.

You know what else is identical? Susie says, you people and a large pile of shit.

If you ask me, says Margot, the real pile of shit is that crackbrained criminal Rumpus.

Well nobody asked you, Susie tells her.

I voted for Trudeau, says Margot.

You're also having sex with a mythological monster who never showers, says Susie. So just zip it.

Take 6: This is Sally Sandcastle, somewhere adrift on the North Atlantic Treaty Organization, searching for discounts on authentic Indian jewelry, lunatic guests, real versus fake breasts, any dirt we can fabricate on the hologram Birdswell, crazy folktales about birds, whatever they might be, and of course Sasquatch, who, according to his live-in housekeeper and part-time lover, Margie Mincemeat, has a really huge ...

Okay, Susie, let's call it a day.

I was about to say intellect.

That has to be a lie.

Fine, say Susie, I don't need you losers. I'll single-handedly find that mine, report it to Brine and then ... on your tiny brains I'll leisurely dine.

Twenty-nine

After a busy morning in front of the mirror, practicing a variety of insane outbursts aimed at solidifying her reputation among the WAGA, WOOGS and WIGWAMS, Malaise Brine changes her underwear (long overdue), once again reminds her reflection that the inevitable reanimation of the The Don is only a matter of time. Which then forces her to think about the word time. She feels certain that she knows what it means. As long as no one asks her to explain it, she'll probably be okay. She suspects that it's only the scientific elitists who insist it's a real thing. Real or otherwise, she has the feeling that whatever time might be, it seems to be creeping along like an old man with arthritis in both knees and a really bad attitude. It's already getting dark before she manages to pull herself away from the mirror.

Earlier, she had finally gotten in touch with Pin Goatfart. Before she could ask his advice on the Rat Gootz situation, Pin began filling her in on the irrefutable proof he now has that North Korean submarines were responsible for bringing in millions of phony democratic votes in exchange for one of the southern states, to be named at a later date. It's the Louisiana Purchase all over again, he insisted. Birdswell has gone too far this time, he shouted into the phone.

Mallory Malaise had to wonder how Pin ever managed to get elected. Of course, Pin Goatfart secretly wonders the same about her. It should have been impossible, which only proves that democracy, when exclusively applied by God-fearing, bigoted Caucasians, sometimes works.

But not to worry, Pin had continued. I've been personally servicing a local faction of the Loud Boys, while at the same time convincing them that saving this great country will require a concerted effort to destroy it.

Amen to that, Malaise Brine had replied. Now when you say servicing ..?

Best not to get into the icky sticky details, Pin had said.

Maybe we can get around to the reason I called? MMB wondered.

Sorry, Brine, said Pin. I'm not dating right now. Nothing personal.

I marginally respect a man who's disinclined to beat around the bush, Malaise Brine said.

Don't really think we should be talking about beating around your bush, said Pin. After all, that's how girls get pregnant.

Mallory briefly imagined being impregnated with Goatfart's semen. She felt her face twist into an expression of uncontrolled disgust, but reminded herself that at least their offspring would never be accused of political correctness.

Anyway, said Pin, all of this will be revealed in my new book, *Abortion Never, Babies Forever.*

Love the title, Mallory Malaise told him, but to be honest, never thought of you as a writer.

Oh, I didn't exactly write it, said Pin. I used that new A.I. writing bot, Bing Crosby.

You know, just recently I was dreaming of a white Christmas.

Yeah, shame it doesn't snow anymore.

Which, as we know, has nothing to do with climate change.

Another leftie lie.

They lie, all we can do is continue to deny.

In fact, a section in my book covers that. Bing Crosby came up with the catchy chapter title, *Climax Exchange for the Deranged.*

Wow! Brine exclaimed.

Pin Goatfart began to sing: *Angry icebergs refuse to melt, fragrant farts I've never smelt, my good pal Brine and her climate-controlled pelt.*

Mallory Malaise had gritted her teeth. How sweet of you to mention me in your book, she said. Can't wait to have my assistant read it, then prepare a two or three word synopsis for me to devour the next time I'm on the toilet.

It's an enticing image, Brine, said Pin. You perched on the bowl becoming intimate with Bing Crosby. But enough about Pin Goatfart and his fantasy life come true. Why are you calling me?

Malaise Brine isn't at all sure that Goatfart's pint-size brain-fizzle on Ratt Gootz was worth the twenty minutes she had been forced to spend on the phone with him. Even worse, after she mentioned Laura-loo Bobsmart's name, she'd had the distinct impression that Goatfart began masturbating. Talk about a slap in the face. Was Laura-loo so much more attractive than she? So what if Laura-loo trimmed her pubic parkland more often than Mallory Malaise did? Start scrubbing away Laura-loo's fake face make up and eventually there'd be nothing left but her screaming skull.

Still, she feels minimally responsible for Ratt. After all, he had been willing to accompany her to that White Nationalist rally in Mississippi. He had also looked extremely sexy in the Nazi Stormtrooper uniform he wore to the post-rally dinner dance.

Ratt Gootz picks up just short of ring number thirty-three. Jeez, Mallory, he says, sounding out of breath. About whatchamacallit. I've been losing my mental mansplain.

Sorry, Ratt, says Mallory. But why are you breathing so hard?

What? No way, I'm not hard.

Is that a crying girl I hear in the background?

Yeah, one of them woke up. Had to tie her to the bed again.

Again?

Hey, didn't want her bolting while I was in the shower.

Anyway, says Malaise, I've been talking with Pin Goatfart.

My condolences.

Yeah, thanks.

What'd he have to say?

Not much that made any sense.

How'd that guy ever get elected?

Jesus only knows.

Well He does claim to know pretty much everything, right?

Thought that was Santa Claus.

Hey, here's a rad thought: Maybe Jesus and Santa are one and the same guy.

That's a movie I'd go see.

Why don't we go together?

You know I'm not dating, right? Just in case my husband decides to come back.

Didn't he walk out like five years ago?

Six, but I've been getting these weird vibes recently, especially when I slip into a semi-see-thru death shroud and start time traveling.

Damn, Brine, might be time for you to throw your bonkers bonnet in the ring.

Just between us, I've got feelers out. More like tentacles, really.

Hey, shut up, Ratt suddenly yells. Can't you see I'm on the phone? Bunch of cry babies.

How many girls did you say are there in the motel room? Malaise asks.

Uh ... not that many, Ratt tells her. So come on, Brine, what's my exit tragedy here?

A couple of bittersweet choices, I'm afraid, says MMB. How do you feel about castration?

What do you mean? Ratt asks. Like going on Glock News and insulting myself?

More like cutting off your own gummy sacks.

Hold on, are you suggesting ..?

Afraid so, the giggle berries got to go.

Wouldn't that make me, like, a woman?

Yeah, you wish. Okay, so forget that. Choice number two, you're gonna have to beat the living crapola out of yourself.

Because ..?

Because you've got to be the victim.

Ah, so the new storyline is that these five to eleven teeny boppers kidnapped me, forced me into this motel room and proceeded to do unspeakable things to me.

That's the plankton, says Mallory, only you're gonna have to go that extra special distance on the physical abuse to prove it.

Not sure I can just beat myself up, says Ratt. Off, no problem, but up?

Just stare at yourself in the mirror for awhile. Half the congress wants to beat you up, based solely on how your face looks.

Yeah, trouble there is that looking at my face usually makes me want to jerk off.

Really sorry you told me that.

And you're really welcome.

All right, so just have the girls do it, Malaise Brine suggests. I have a feeling they won't mind kicking the putrid pudding out of you.

Fucking brilliant, Brine, howls Ratt. I only wish you were here to get in on the action.

Yeah, I almost wish that, too, Malaise tells him.

Thirty

Mollie Millicent, President Birdswell's Tuesday/Thursday advisor on all matters that hardly mattered, enters the polyhedron office on a pair of crisply delicate feet, wearing a purple jumpsuit; as purple is the President's favorite T-days color.

Ah, Millipede, says Birdswell. I've been sitting here wondering what I should be doing ... and now I know.

And what is that, Mister President? Mollie asks.

Waiting for you.

And here I am, says Mollie.

And not a tick of the clack too soon. What's on the veranda?

A couple of things, sir.

A couple? says Birdswell, as in ..?

Well, two.

Excellent. Safety in numbers, as they say.

They do say that, don't they?

Shall we take it from the top?

Of course, says Mollie, opening her notepad. First, we're getting increasingly concerning reports on outbreaks of blathering.

Ah, blathering outbreaks, eh?

Yes Sir.

Blather, blather, soap and lather.

Debate on your *Save the Seagull* bill had to be suspended, as Senators Crust and Mayhem descended into a blathering screaming match.

Those two idiots have been incomprehensible since long before the blathering got started.

Mollie nods. Crust claimed that seagulls were actually bumblebees, with knees, while Mayhem claimed we need giant space nets to stop all alien sea creatures from entering the nation's forbidden land masses.

Birdswell laughs. Sorry I wasn't there to see that.

It went on, Sir. Crust called Mayhem a gerrymandering moron on a merry-go-round; Mayhem countered by referring to Crust as a Corpus Christi caterpillar who hides in the underpants of pedophiles.

Pretty much on the money, says Birdswell. Although I wasn't aware that pedophiles wore underpants.

It does seem counterintuitive, Mister President, Mollie says.

You're thinking espionage, Multifaceted?

Only if we're willing to consider the many worlds theory, says Mollie.

So, while I'm talking with you in this world, I'm taking a bath in another, having a nap in yet another?

And in yet another, we've already decided that there is no such thing as a many worlds theory.

You never fail to stimulate my mental implants, Minerva.

Your words fall on tentatively tumultuous ears, Mister President.

I am a married man, Birdswell reminds her. And I'm no Ronaldo McDonald Rumpus.

Mollie blushes. Moving on, Sir. Doctor's Mellmack and Portmanteau are here to brief you on ... let me get this right ... *matters of reality-melding, molten-masticating, lethally lugubrious, world importance.*

Sounds like something one of those triple A motor bots would cook up. The italics are pretty much a death-rattling give-away.

Well, neither of them appears particularly humanistic, Mister President.

Some sort of newfangled technology?

If aliens were real, I might be inclined to say ... you know.

Do I?

Aliens, Mister President.

Jesus Lord of Gumption.

Amen, says Mollie, crossing herself.

Tell me this, Madelene, is it by any chance nap time?

Sorry, Mister President. Not for another two twinkles and a slow-motion wink.

Oh well. Suppose you'd better bring them in.

Mellmack and Portmanteau, impersonating a pair of reluctant shadows, slip into the oddly angled office, clearly looking the part of lunatics pretending to be scientists. Mellmack in crumpled tweed, eyebrows exploding like an expanding universe over the edges of his glasses. Portmanteau in dirty jeans and a tee-shirt, across the front of which is written *Depraved For Science.* While Mellmack has an Einstein-like jumble of white hair on his head, Portmanteau had adopted the retro hairstyle of the Mohawk Indian.

Mister President, Mellmack bellows, his voice oddly pitched and quavering. Thank you for attempting to hypnotize us.

Nonsense, says Birdswell. There's always time on my schedule for scientology.

Portmanteau is about to correct the President, but Mellmack shoots him a *don't even bother* facial expression.

No doubt you boys are quite busy in the lavatory, Birdswell tells them.

Mellmack again glares at Portmanteau. Particularly with all the unprecedented hoopla occurring around us, he says.

Hoopla, muses Birdswell. No ifs ands or buts about that.

Let's just say a few nagging buts have come up, answers Mellmack.

Not to mention an if or two, adds Portmanteau.

In any case, says Birdswell, I'm gratified you boys found the time to make a disappearance.

In fact, says Portmanteau, we initially intended to send you the data using a form of aerial transportation.

Yes, Mellmack continues, but unfortunately we could not verify the actual existence of said transport mode.

That is to say, continues Portmanteau, we had a word for it in our heads, but no corresponding data on its possible reality.

And what word is that? Birdswell wonders.

Pigeon, Mellmack and Portmanteau answer in unison.

Pig-eon, the President repeats the word. It's a new one on me. How about it, Mistress Melanie? he presumably asks Mollie.

Mollie scrunches up her eyes, hotly scans her memory, initializing a deep dive word search. Possibly some sort of winged creature from a purely mythological past? she offers.

Both Mellmack and Portmanteau nod, again in unison.

Ah, the good old days, says Birdswell. Anyway, maybe you fellas should just go ahead and hit me with the bad news first.

Actually, says Portmanteau, all we have is bad news with which to hit you.

Bummer, whistles Birdswell. Well, we best get on with it, cause in precisely ... *he looks at Mollie, she checks her watch, remembers it stopped working several units of something or other ago, does a quick mental calculation, then holds up one finger, two fingers and five fingers ...* one hundred twenty-five years, I'll be heading in for a nap.

Mollie giggles, causing Portmanteau to also giggle. Obviously, she says, the President means one hundred and twenty-five millibars of mercury.

Impressive that you remember all the M words, Missy, Birdswell tells her.

Both Mellmack and Portmanteau also appear visibly impressed.

A lengthy silent pause ensues. No one in the room seems to notice it.

Finally, Mellmack pipes up. In a nutshell, Mister President, it's the entropy.

I had no idea you weren't well, Birdswell tells him. As I recall, that particular ailment is mostly terminal.

So wrong, ponders Portmanteau, and at the same time, so right.

And you caught it from eating nuts, you say? Birdswell asks.

No, Mellmack says. I refer to the arrow of time.

Birdswell looks at Mollie, she shrugs, making a *who the fuck knows* face.

If I may, announces Portmanteau, entropy is the irreversible process in a system from order to disorder. Basically, disorder in the universe is always increasing.

Pretty much the same situation going on in my head, says Birdswell.

Paradoxically, Portmanteau continues, entropy is critical for life as we know it.

Indeed, Mellmack says, think of us as currently existing within the ideal entropic window.

Portmanteau retakes the floor. Unfortunately, says he, our calculations suggest that entropy had reversed itself, and ...

... is now running backwards, Mellmack finishes his sentence.

Backwards running now is, echoes Portmanteau.

President Birdswell appears to have dozed off.

What exactly does this mean? Mollie asks.

We wish we knew, says Mellmack.

Safe to say, says Portmanteau, we're running out of possibilities, stuck in a what-happened-to-all-the-crazy-information situation.

We may experience a slowing down, or even a complete stoppage, of temerity, says Mellmack.

We might begin repeating everything, in an endlessly recurring loop-de-loop, says Portmanteau.

Our hungry brains may begin to invent all matter of absurd nonsense, offers Mellmack, just so that we have something to do.

Outside chance we all become immortal, Portmanteau adds.

Or simply enter a perpetual state of extreme slow-motion dying, says a frowning Mellmack.

Huh, says Mollie. So pretty much what's already happening.

Both scientists appear confused.

Sorry, says Mellmack, but we don't get out much.

Do you think these incidents of blathering, mass migrations and the bizarre rumors of telepathic exsanguination could all be somehow related? Mollie asks.

Did we mention the entropy thing? Portmanteau asks.

Mellmack stands up, begins walking backwards across the room. I'd say that link positively stinks, he says.

There's irony in them thar hills, says Portmanteau. The increasingly empty brain space resulting from a low entropy dust up seems to be particularly susceptible to whatever cockamamie gibber-quiver is being cooked up in the pressurized skullcaps of the grossly misinformed.

Think of blathering as a spicy side dish, best served at a temperature of absolute zero, says Mellmack.

So is that a yes? Mollie asks.

Short answer, says Mellmack.

But anything, and also nothing, is possible now, says Portmanteau.

Hold on, says Mollie, one of you is wondering what color underwear I'm wearing.

Has to be him, says Mellmack, pointing at Portmanteau.

Purple, right? says a smiling Portmanteau,

You're such a multi-personality piglet, Mollie tells him.

Is the President dead? Mellmack wonders.

The dead can neither die, lie nor tie their own shoes, says Portmanteau.

The pie is hidden in my bed, says Mollie. I enjoy eating it while reclining in the nude.

Any chance you've posted that video on Instagram? Portmanteau asks.

And what about the cow? Mellmack wonders.

In orbit around the make believe moon? Mollie offers.

I can't remember the last time I peed, says Portmanteau.

I've always wanted to play Ring Around the Rosie, says Mellmack.

I, too, am plagued with images of sauerkraut, says Portmanteau.

Thank you, gentle ladies, says Mollie. The President will almost certainly refuse to see you now, or ever again.

Thirty-one

Hello and good evening, or morning, based upon your current geopolitical orientation. This is Trixie Sonnenborg, coming to you, either dead or alive, from an undisclosed studio location. You may notice I'm whispering. Quite unlike my usually bubbling, outspoken, confrontational persona. Let's just say that, based on our last live show, I've been warned by the powers that be. Of course, no one actually knows who these so-called powers are, but apparently it's not beyond their Ken to have me simply erased. Me, the postmodern Barbie herself. You may also notice that my usually lively, borderline boisterous, live studio audience has been replaced with a number of strategically placed robots, interspersed with a variety of cardboard cut-outs modeled on a typically Trixie Sonnenborg bio-diverse audience.

Trixie pauses for a drink.

Only water in this cup, my friends; also part of the new protocol. No more hallucinogenic laced lime juice for this prime time hostess. In addition, during tonight's program you will not hear me utter even a single profanity. It has been pointed out to me that my reliance on these words, in particular the *F*-word, is contrary to the interest of the family-based values this network wishes to espouse. Whatever the *F* that means?

Apologies to our Born Again Christian sponsors, and to the manufacturers of *Abortion-less,* the non-natural, highly toxic remedy for all those silly teen ladies who have mistakenly taken the after sex abortion pill. With *Abortion-less,* you're guaranteed to be once again carrying that little bundle of major misery to term.

Muted applause.

Now on to our very special guest this evening, and I don't have to tell you the number of times I had to put out in order to get him, or her, or it, on the show. Suffice it to say, this is a first. Never before seen, heard or smelt. Now, due to the highly secretive nature of this guest's identity, he/she/it will only appear as a figment of our mostly depleted imaginations.

Of course, we've all heard the rumors, and many of us have believed these strange notions in our heads are examples of original thought, and we called ourselves parched prophets and pro-life proselytizers of a new world disorder. We've seen the strange lights in the sky, even as the current administration denies, defies and spews out lies. I'm talking aliens, folks. And one of them is here tonight to counter all the phony propaganda, the false flags and interstellar dogwhistles. The aliens are with us, people, whether we like it or not, and it's high time our leaders face up to it. Sure, we're most likely doomed, but that doesn't mean we can't milk the situation for all it's worth for as long as we can.

Slightly more enthusiastic applause.

First off, mysterious guest, what would you like to be called? Do you have a preferred pronoun, an alien call sign, perhaps?

A crackling noise, followed by s series of hisses and scratchy metal sounds.

Forgive me, Taxi, a robotic voice says. Our universal translator interface still has a few blogs, as you bug people like to say.

Uh ... not a problem, says Trixie, thinking it could very well be a problem.

You may call me Your Exalted Highness, if you like, or simply Mister Friendly.

Your Exalted Highness sounds a tad highfalutin, so I'll just go with Mister Friendly. And please call me Trixie, rather than Taxi.

I could of course call you a taxi, Trixie.

Not necessary, Mister Friendly. So, just to set the record straight, you are real.

As opposed to unreal.

And exactly how many of you are there.

There is only one of me, Trixie.

I mean others of your ... ilk.

None of my others drink milk.

And your kind, are there hundreds, thousands, millions?

We rarely count above ten.

Okay then. If I may ask, Mister Friendly - and needless to say your answer to this question is something my audience is extremely eager to hear - what is your mission?

More high-pitched crackling, followed by a sustained whining sound.

Sorry, that word does not compute, screeches Mister Friendly.

In other words, says Trixie, why are you here?

A lengthy pause, distant chattering.

Our consensus is that we are here because we are not elsewhere.

Do you intend to conquer the planet Earth?

It is our belief that the inhabitants of your world are much too stupid to deserve our intervention. We are simply here to enjoy the crazy show.

So answer me this, Mister Friendly, how do you explain all the weird goings on? The delusions, the mass gatherings, the blathering, the telepathic tadpoles?

We refer you to our previous answer.

Okay, says Trixie, quick answer, if you please. Are you in cahoots with the radical democrats, as zillions of American amoebas currently believe?

A loud humming noise.

In cahoots, says Mister Friendly. From the French *cahute*, suggesting cabins and huts.

Yes, that's all very interesting, says Trixie, but ...

A buzzer goes off, followed by what sounds a lot like a dentist's drill.

Related words, Mister Friendly continues: allied, affiliated, associated, hooked up, plugged in.

Are you perhaps admitting that you and President Birdswell have hooked up?

Birds tend to be unreliable, Trixie, and yes, all is well with me. How about you?

Honestly, I could use a drink.

I myself enjoy a tall cool glass of engine oil, with a few lumps of space ice.

Sounds delicious.

Yessiree Bob! I just learned this expression and wanted to try it out.

And you used it perfectly.

Thanks a million for saying so.

Okay, so what's the story with the moon?

An unreliable rock in close earth orbit.

I regularly receive thoughts that the moon is little more than an expired egg, as viewed through a magician's magnifying teacup.

The lighted side of the moon is an illusion, the dark side is home to a billion bumblebees.

So you admit there are alien biases on a harvest moon, says Trixie.

There is no alien hypocrisy in this vector of space, says Mister Friendly.

Aren't you an alien?

From our perspective, you are the alien, Trixie.

But I've never been to the moon, Trixie says. The last time I looked up at it, I starting howling.

I could take you, says Mister Friendly. I know a great restaurant. Do you like fresh rodent sushi?

What should we in the media, responsible for speaking in honeycombed platitudes, say to the people of Earth?

There is a popular earth expression that I particularly enjoy.

And what might that be?

Go fuck yourself.

A siren goes off, this one inside the studio.

I'm very sorry, Mister Friendly, but you can't say that on live TV.

Say what?

The *F* word, obviously.

A loud honking sound.

F words, says Mister Friendly. As in: frugal, fabulous, flamboyant, fascist, feminine, feeble-minded ...

Fuck, Trixie screams.

And now a word from our sponsor:

We've all been there, ladies. Deluding ourselves that we're in love, agreeing to the demands of some pimply nitwit, who by the way forgot to buy condoms, but you do it anyway, probably appalled at how bad it was, and then you start to panic, have your big sister drive you to the pharmacy, where you buy that ugly abortion pill, just in case; and then the next day you wake up, riddled with guilt, feeling like a murderer and a monster, crying your eyes out, praying to God, just wishing there was some way to take it all back ...

And now there is.

Say hello to *Abortion-less*, the little pink pill guaranteed to put that baby bump back in you underaged belly. Talk to your family doctor today. And if, by chance, he tells you that you're much too young to become a mother, you have the permission of both republicans and religious zealots to kill him.

One *Abortion-less* pill only $1257.00, wherever quality drugs are sold.

Tell me, asks Mister Friendly, are all you humans hopelessly insane?

Based on that commercial alone, Trixie tells him, I'd have to say yes. You should probably just go ahead and incinerate the planet.

But before that, I'd really like to go Trick-or-Treating with you, Trixie.

Okay, I have to get out of here, Trixie says. Can somebody please call me a taxi?

You're a taxi, Trixie, booms over the studio speakers.

Or perhaps you would prefer a ride in my spaceship? Mister Friendly inquires.

No strings attached, right? Trixie asks.

Unless you'd care to call our quantum anti-matter hyper-engines strings, says Mister Friendly.

So like string theory, right? Says Trixie.

Sure, says Mister Friendly, but good luck trying to prove it.

This is Trixie Sonnenborg, signing off and also leaving Earth, hopefully forever. My final words of advice for all of you out there, wherever you are ... say it wth me Mister Friendly .....

Go fuck Yourselves!

Loud sustained applause. Several robots in the audience join in. Many of the human facsimile cardboard cutouts burst into flame.

Thirty-two

Karla, backstage, adding the finishing touches to her look: face firmly in place, silicon-filled wrinkles invisible, snake-eye contacts correctly glaring, wig, woven from the hair of one of her former political rivals, looking about as perfectly arranged as a slice of her favorite blueberry pie on a plate. She is slim, trim and ready for the jungle gym; a svelte cat on the prowl, a crusader, a warrior of alternative truth, a big fat bullshitter, a promoter of the gargantuan lie ... *hold on, cut those last two bits. No sense giving the baby away with the toilet water.*

Good one, Karla, she tells herself, heading for the stage. Feel free to use it if the opportunity presents itself.

Applause as she steps to the podium. First two rows reserved for members of the press. Behind them a medium-size group of supporters: overweight middle age men who enjoy fantasizing about Karla naked, overweight middle age women looking like they haven't slept in several weeks, a small but fervid group from the local Christian coalition, *Hand-jobs for Jesus.* Placards proclaim: *As a holy alternative to the sin of premarital penetration.*

Karla glares at the crowd, her thinnish lips coated in blood red lipstick, her posture not adversely affected by the six inch heals she's wearing.

How perfectly petrified you all look, says Karla. Terrified of the corruption that dogs us like a demon's diarrhea. We've had enough, right?

A smattering of hoots and hollers.

We're ready to stand up, scream at the top of our lungs, No more, goddammit! Excuse my profanity, but I've had it up to here.

Karla karate-chops her own forehead, staggers back a few steps, before correcting herself.

Now what do we know? she asks.

That Jesus never jerks off, shouts someone in the audience.

Yes, that's true, says a nodding Karla. Because Jesus is a good boy, and listens to his Mommy when she tells him, *Never Touch Your Weeny, unless it's a real-life emergency!*

Someone begins beating a drum.

Thank you, says Karla, to all our native American brothers and sisters. Even if you weren't allowed into the auditorium today, we stand with you. Long live the Little Big Horn!

Someone blows a horn.

Karla walks back and forth, like a cooped up hyena.

And we also know that our election was stolen. The deep dark state crept in, no doubt with the help of the Asians and the Aliens, and snatched victory away from us. At this very moment, the radial cosplayer Betty *Bland* Bumpkins sits on the Governor's commode, wearing my clothes, eating my snacks. Enough! And do you know what?

What, Karla? Someone shouts.

Well I'll tell you, man with the bright red nose and the bad breath I can smell all the way up here. Stealing the election wasn't enough for them. No sir. They also stole my husband's erection. Flaccid as uncooked pizza dough since election day. Any wonder I'm a nervous wreck?

Several women in the audience open their mouths, issue a barely audible squeaking sound.

I'll tell you this, though, Karla continues, we will never stop fighting. Currently we have one hundred and thirty-seven active lawsuits filed, as well as a petition, signed by over eleven diehard supporters, and mailed directly to the King of Patagonia. I also have it on good authority that no less a super-luminary then the Pope himself has said, and I quote, *Karla Lacky has a perfidious cracky.* Still waiting for the original latin translation of that, but let's face it people, God is clearly on our side.

Applause, the banging of Bibles together, producing small clouds of God-adulterated dust.

And now I'll take a few questions from the media, none of whom here today representing the left wing fake news, or the fake flowers of leftist leftovers, or the moldy tombs of communist lunatics.

A man in the front row raises his hand. Karla points at his head, her eyes sending a freezing shiver straight down into his britches.

Speaking of moldy tombs, Karla, are you confident that former President Rumpus will be successfully reanimated in time to finally destroy the world? And if not, will you be throwing your cobweb-coated veil in the ring?

Karla stretches the limits of her mouth, activating several throbbing veins in her temples. I can tell you, in confidence, that I am in near-constant contact with the President's non-retarded son, Roscoe, who assures me that it's only a matter of God's good timely nonsense before The Don retakes his place upon the royal toilet.

Is it true that Planka originally opposed her father's reanimation?

Karla smirks, her tongue poking between pursed lips. Planka Moremoney is the classic definition of Far East Coast snobbery and self-indulgence. She spends more money on underwear than the gross national product of Pakistan. In addition, she possesses the loyalty of a spoiled sea turtle. Once President Rumpus regains his status and stamina, it wouldn't surprise me one bit if he took Planka over his knee and spanked her bare bottom. Repeatedly.

Another hand from the press section:

Do you enjoy a bare bottom spank now and then, Karla?

Let me answer that by saying only that I'm a human woman with all the needs and urges of your average North Dakotan nymphomaniac.

It has been reported in a well-respected New York City newspaper that you may not be completely human. Care to comment, Karla?

First, says Karla, let me say that I have nothing but pity for the shitty stain known as New York City. And if I am not completely human, it's only because I'm partly divine.

More Bible thwacking, a rising chant from the religious right:

Karla and Jesus sitting in a tree, k-i-s-s-i-n-g. First comes love, then comes marriage, then come's a hand job behind the baby carriage.

But seriously, Karla, if The Don decides to re-toss his hairpiece into the ring, would you consider becoming his number two in the next installment of presidential felonies and abuses of power?

Needless to say, says Karla, it would be an honor and a privilege to join President Rumpus on his new reality TV show, *Live From The Bigfoot Lair Bathroom.* However, as I have repeatedly said, by next Thursday at 3:35 PM, I expect to be snuggled up like a bug in a rug in the king-size bed inside the Governor's mansion, proclaiming a new national holiday in honor of holy retribution, American style.

A second chant rising up:

Some will say only fools don't pray, unless of course you're communist or gay, but we're here to tell you this today, the USA is here to stay..

Sorry to say, Ms. Lackey, but by all accounts, you actually lost the election by eleven million votes, in a state with only twelve million eligible voters.

I'm sure you've all seen the recent documentary special on the undead voters, led by a mythical forest creature, and the assembly line of fake vote production somewhere beneath the giant Canadian ice cream cone. By our estimation, five million semi-dead bodies swarmed the polling booths in our great state alone on election day. And by the way, I have it on good authority that the current fake governor Betty Bumpkins is secretly married to an undocumented Guatemalan zombie.

Do you have the support of Mallory Malaise Brine, Karla?

Let me just say that Malaise Brine and I are like two muckraking mares at a Bible Belt barn burning, says Karla. I was at her side the day she exposed Filaria Fulton as the ringleader of the pizza parlor pedophiles.

Chanting: *Praise the holy pie, the truth is in the lie, all demoncrats must die die die.*

And I'll let you in on a little secret, says a winking Karla. Malaise Brine, Laura-loo Bobsmart and I have had more than a few all-girl sleepovers, during which not everyone was wearing pajamas in bed.

Thirty-three

Good evening to all of you still out there, those of you at least minimally in touch with the last remnants of reality, with a lingering smudge of faith in B.S. News to explain just how implausible things have become. This is Bright Silversperm, against all odds, in the studio, with possible real-life zombies at the door and at least one homicidal killer on the payroll. There have been death threats, people. Here's one I received within the last five to a million temporal units.

Hey Silversperm, I'm gonna stretch your mouth open with a car jack, then push a canister of napalm down your throat. As soon as you're well done, I intend to eat both your eyeballs and your testicles.

And this was one of the more reasonable threats.

Anyway, despite the fact that all the clocks have been running backwards at an dizzying rate, as well as the unfortunate circumstance of most of us here in the B.S. studio now wholeheartedly believing in what's being called *The Inevitable Uprising of the Lizard People*, we feel the news must go on. Neither sleet, nor hail, nor Mary's holy moly emoji will keep us from our disappointing task.

Pause ...

Apologies. Just trying to recall if I took out my trash this morning, or whether I'll find a host of fetid ghosts engaged in after-death hijinks in my kitchen when I get home. Assuming getting home is still an option. And trust me, people, even a grown man with something less than a bone-crushing anxiety disorder, is still capable of wetting the bed. And I'm not talking tinkle tinkle little star, either. When an adult man on the cusp of obesity releases his bladder while asleep in his bed, the result is comparable to a gigantic Slip & Slide in a Silicon Valley Mega-mall.

But enough of my overwrought balderdash. As you may have heard, our beloved and yes, often despised, Dave Darwin has either been confined to a mental hospital for the incurably insane, or kidnapped by angry aliens, possibly in cahoots with the above mentioned Lizard People. Basically a *you pick-um* situation. Either way, highly unlikely that Dave will be rejoining us anytime soon.

So basically it's come down to Silversperm or no sperm at all. And good luck, ladies, getting pregnant with that guy.

Okay, I'm being informed by one of my producers - *and just between you and me, the maniac murderer alluded to earlier could very well be him* - that all but one hundred and eleven of you have just switched off your TVs, with an expression of barely disguised revulsion upon your faces. Well, fuck all of you, then ...

Sorry, Charles. Meant to say ... well, suckle the balls of that hen. Yes, Charles, that is a real expression. Check the internet if you don't believe me. Seriously? The internet's not real, either?

In any case, speaking of all things unsavory, it's requiring a lot right now for me to relinquish the spotlight and announce that our newest Asian Wunderkind is about to go live somewhere in southeastern Oklahoma, or possibly northwestern Arkansas, one of those states nobody believes actually exist, anticipating the arrival of the mass march of the debunked, the disenfranchised and the severely debilitated, direct through the north by northwest corridor, it's origin speculated to be somewhere in the even less probable state of Idaho.

Candace Wong, can you hear me? It's Bright Silversperm.

We hear the annoyed-sounding voice of Candace: I'm sorry, Brent Silver-what? That can't be a real name.

Bright tries again: Candace? Our massive national audience awaits your report with baited and no doubt extremely odious breath.

Candace continues speaking to someone at her location: I refuse to talk to anyone with sperm in his last name. And no, I don't care what color it is.

Bright: Candace, the entire world can hear you.

Candace: Bottom line, I hate sperm. The first time I laid eyes on it, I instantly became a lesbian.

Bright: No doubt we'd all love to hear the details of that encounter.

Candace: Well, if you know someone in the studio willing to do it, give him the go-ahead. What? The studio killer's a her?

Bright: Oh My God!

Candace: All right, fine. But if this goes ass-sideways, you and I will definitely not be sharing a bed at the motel tonight.

Bright: Thought she was a lesbian. Say what? Her on-site producer is a woman?

Hello, Bright? Can you hear me? Candace Wong here.

Oh, Candace, there you are.

I sure am, Bright.

Can you fill us in on what's happening out about where you are, Candace?

Well, we're standing here on the precipice, the eternal edge of nothingness, you might even say, awaiting the arrival of what is reputed to be the largest, ugliest and most deranged mass exodus since Moses led the money-lenders out of the black death and into the blue dawn of the Desert Sands Casino Hotel.

Wow, says Bright. Talk about sneaking bad poetry into an implausible news report. Not entirely sure about that Moses thing-a-ma-bob, either, but whatever ...

Read your Bible sometime, Bright, says Candace.

Don't expect you'll be doing much of that back at the motel this evening, Candace. You and Patty Periwinkle, I mean.

Sorry, Bright, Patty who?

You know, your twenty year old producer, with the perfect skin, minor miracle tits and a can that just won't quit.

Not that it's any of your beeswax, Bright boy, but her name's Brenda.

Hold it the hell on, Bright cries. Susie Metcalfe said what now?

Bright? Are you still there?

Sorry, Candy-corn, but one of our assistant's here in the studio is most likely a homicidal maniac.

Oh, you mean Susie?

You know Susie?

Of course I know Susie.

Well, any advise on how to handle her?

Whatever you do, Bright, don't beg for your life. She hates that.

Thirty-four

Jane and Mickelmoose reach the prescribed blood/brain barrier, under cloudy skies, with the mingling aromas of pizza and petrochemicals in the air. Another squad car has reached the barrier before them, the vehicle wedged between an apparent rock and a hard place. Jane is not thrilled to see that it's occupied by Santini and his dumbbell doppelgänger Reindeer, two of the absolute worst cops in the entire regional four state dustbowl.

Talk about two cops on the terminal takeout line, sneers Mickelmoose.

As I understand it, says Jane, Santini's uncle is pretty much the number two boss bitch of the Tulsa Tough Boys.

It don't get much worse than them, says Mickelmoose.

Reindeer's the perfect patsy for that little party, says Jane.

Rusty Reindeer's sort of famous, though, says Mickelmoose.

How so? Jane wants to know.

He scored the lowest I.Q. on the entrance exam of any cop ever accepted into the ranks, says Mickelmoose.

Based on the people we work with, says Jane, it's got to be pretty damn low.

How low can a reindeer go? Mickelmoose muses.

Suppose we'd better go link up with the goon squad, says Jane, reaching for her door handle and exiting the vehicle.

Hey, Jankowitz, says Santini, thought you'd be home done up like a mannequin for Yom Kippur.

That's not what your mommy said last night, Santini, says Mickelmoose.

Santini pulls his service weapon, pokes Mickelmoose in the chest with it. You saying my mommy's a mannequin?

Okay, says Jane, let's all relax. And by the way, Santini, I have it on good authority that Jesus definitely didn't die for your sins.

That's count one of religious discrimination, Jankowitz, says Santini, crossing himself.

Hey, Santini, says Mickelmoose, how's your uncle, the one-legged sex-trafficking pimp?

Better than your old man, Moose breath, replies Santini. Heard he's camping outside the bus station, offering blow jobs for a dollar a pop?

Hey, says Mickelmoose, the economy's in a recession, in case you hadn't noticed.

A distant rumble, far-off what could be chanting.

What the hell is that? Santini asks.

What we're here to find out, Jane tells him.

Could be a million heading our way, says Mickelmoose.

Yeah, says Santini, but a million what?

Reindeer finally breaks his silence. I heard some of them are lizard look-a-likes who feast on the rotting remains of human desperation.

Where'd that come from? Mickelmoose wants to know.

It's in my head, says Reindeer, pointing to his head.

Anything in there about birds? Mickelmoose asks.

Reindeer screams.

You deliberately trying to scare the kid? Santini wants to know.

Look, says Jane, far as we know they're just folks, no doubt low on the smarts, who have somehow lost their way.

So Reindeer's entire family is most likely among them. Santini laughs.

Is among right? Mickelmoose wonders. Or would it be amongst?

When the undead come a calling, recites Reindeer, it's no time for stalling.

Okay, says Santini, answer me this, Sargent Spank-My-Bottom. There's only four of us. How are we supposed to hold off a million loons under the weight of this here full moon?

That moon ain't real, says Reindeer.

I'm looking right at it, says Santini.

Hold on, says Mickelmoose, don't jump down the kid's throat. I've been having my doubts about it, too.

If it's any help, says Jane, my mother's convinced it's made of toilet paper.

I heard Rumpus stole every single roll of toilet paper in the entire D.C. metro area, says Santini.

The guy stole everything else, says Mickelmoose, why not the toilet paper?

I once wiped my ass with exotic ostrich feathers, says Reindeer.

Jane throws him a disparaging glance. Getting back to the original query, she says ....

You mean what came first, the Big Bang, or God's first fart? (*This probably courtesy of Santini; small chance from an as yet unidentified fifth party*)

I heard a big bang once, says Reindeer. Darn near struck me down dead in a barnyard-full of unhappy corpses.

What I was going to say, Jane continues, we're not going to confront these people, or whatever they are. We'll talk to them, try to persuade them to detour our town. Also, we've been authorized to offer each of them one free coupon for an evening of Big Time Bingo in an adjoining state to be named at a later date.

Yeah, snickers Santini, the state of disbelief.

Or non-existence, says Reindeer.

The other three stare at him.

How do we even know we're real? Reindeer asks.

I've been having the feeling that this, whatever this is, only started sometime last week, says Mickelmoose.

Yeah, says Santini, the past is a hopelessly distorted memory stick, the future an impossible family reunion.

Are you listening to yourselves? Jane asks.

The others shake their heads.

I'll tell you this, says Santini, as I see it, we've got two options. We shoot first and ask meaningless questions later, or we hide somewhere until they pass.

Let me ask you, says Jane, how long do you think it will take for a million quasi-living crawlers to go past our current location?

Got to be a couple of light years, says Mickelmoose.

A light year is a measure of distance, says Reindeer.

So answer me this, says Mickelmoose, exactly how heavy is one of these so-called light years?

Anyway, says Reindeer, if we assume an average walking speed of five miles an hour, and a mass equivalent to half the state of Rhode Island, we can estimate it will take them approximately 3.7 months to pass this location.

I thought you said he was dumb, Jane says.

He is, says Santini. That's just the sort of shit dumb people think about.

Maybe he's a savant, says Mickelmoose.

Yeah, or maybe a shoe salesman on the side, say Santini.

Or a shaman who sells seashells, cries Reindeer.

I think we all need to take a step back, says Jane.

Everyone takes a step back.

I actually enjoyed that, says Mickelmoose.

Okay, my final option, says Santini. We tell them to scram. If they refuse, we call in the jets.

A perennial middle of the standings football team? a visibly confused Mickelmoose asks.

The rumbling is suddenly closer, mild tremors agitate the ground beneath them, an almost fathomable chant.

Listen, says Jane, cupping her ears with her hands.

Malaise Brine, her furry green, the time to scream, got hard in a dream, Mallory Malaise, screwed in a haze, fell out of faze, came in her own daze ...

Disgusting, if true, says Mickelmoose.

Sounds a bit like an all-night sex party I attended one time in Cincinnati, says Santini.

Jane senses the steady siphoning off of information, realizes she knows less now about the situation than she did before they arrived. Assuming they have arrived. Do any of you recall why we're here? she asks.

Mickelmoose and Santini shrug; then, for reasons never fully acknowledged, hug.

I believe we're here to witness the end, says Reindeer.

The end of what? Jane asks.

The end of ... this run-on sentence? says Reindeer.

The end of my shift would be even better, says Santini.

All right, says Mickelmoose, enough with the third degree. So big deal if I occasionally wet the bed.

I think we need more intel, says Jane, removing the taser from her belt. She holds it up to her ear. Hello dog patch, she whispers, come in.

You should probably reverse the charges on that, suggests Santini.

Who are you people? Mickelmoose wants to know.

I was a cereal eater in a previous life, says Reindeer.

Previous life, or previously a midwife? Santini asks.

Mickelmoose sings: *That old midwife crisis has me in its spell.*

Jane considers using her taser phone on Mickelmoose, decides instead to replace it on her belt. She returns to the group.

Any joy? Someone asks. No telling who.

Reindeer giggles. What is joy but a deplorable ploy of the capitalist overshoes?

Not sure a questioning shark is needed there, says Mickelmoose.

Apparently, says Jane, we are facing a worst case scenario.

Don't tell me, says Santini. No more free drugs from the evidence locker?

Hold on, says Mickelmoose, what month is it?

Everyone looks at their watches, shakes their heads.

My girlfriend snores after sex, Jane tells them.

Mine is made of plastic, and often claims to have a headache, says Reindeer.

I once had sexual relations with my great aunt Ida's ghost, Mickelmoose admits.

Santini again draws his weapon. Sorry, he announces, but I'm revising our only option option.

The others wait to hear what this new option option might be.

Thirty-five

Oh my God! Planka moans.

What the hell is that? squeals Egbert.

It's just Tammy's blood, Roscoe tells them.

Flashback:

Tammy being chased around the sarcophagus, finally snared and held down by Planka and Egbert.

Jesus, says Planka to Egbert, you really stink.

Don't blame me that our ancient astronauts never showered.

Just don't let her move, says Roscoe, closing in, hunting knife in hand.

Tammy wails. You three assholes have always hated me.

We've also always hated each other, says Planka.

Roscoe grabs Tammy's arm, positions the blade over a throbbing artery.

Stop this now, screams Tammy, and I'll give all three of you a blowjob.

Can a girl give a blowjob to another girl? Egbert wonders.

All the blowjobs in China can't save you now, Tammy, says Planka.

The knife pierces Tammy's skin, her scream sending a reverberating shudder throughout the crypt.

Flash forward:

Why in the name of daddy's eleven pornstar mistresses is her blood green? Planka asks.

No idea, says Roscoe. Maybe she was preconceived on Saint Patrick's Day.

He chased all the elephants out of Ireland, says Egbert.

For your information, claims a weeping Tammy, I happen to be on my period.

Hardly see this as a punctuation issue, says Roscoe.

What color is your poop? Planka wants to know.

I've got it, Egbert shouts. Our half-sister is an alien.

Or maybe one of the lizard people, says Roscoe.

I'm thinking of selling lizard people lookalikes on my website, says Planka. In real leather, needless to say.

Are you saying our father had sex with a creature from outer space? Tammy wants to know.

Trust me, says Planka, if it had a pussy, he grabbed for it.

Did he grab yours, too? Tammy asks Planka.

Planka rolls her eyes, involuntarily squeezing her thighs together.

Anyway, says Roscoe, none of this matters one hootenanny. We've got enough blood, let's get to the ritual.

Think we could maybe have a snack first? Egbert asks.

And how about a band-aid? Tammy asks.

I should probably call Morty, says Planka. Tell him to warm up the hyperbaric chamber pot for me.

Why don't you just divorce that robotic rodent? Roscoe asks.

I refer you to my married name, says Planka.

What's her married name? Tammy asks.

Egbert shrugs. And who knew she had her very own time machine?

Look, says Roscoe, we're on a tight schedule here. Between blood letting and ritualistic dancing and chanting, there is no time out for either food or first aid.

For once I agree with Roscoe, says Planka. The sooner we get this over with, the sooner I can get the fuck out of here and begin a serious, week-long detox.

Planka said the *F* word, Egbert giggles.

Great, says Roscoe. So here's the plan. The three of you will dance around daddy's crypt, chanting, while I apply the blood.

Sounds like you got the easy job, Egbert says to his brother.

Hardly, Roscoe tells him, considering the blood has to be applied with precision, according to the ancient texts, recently procured by me from a world-famous museum that will remain unnamed to avoid yet another lawsuit.

You mean those ancient texts over there, a pointing Planka asks.

None of your business, Roscoe tells her, but yes.

Funny that they look so much like comic books, says Planka.

You've always been a troublemaker, Planka, says Roscoe.

And a bubble breaker, adds Egbert.

She once tried to put me out with the rubbish, says Tammy.

Let's just agree that I'm a bitch, and move on, says Planka.

All those in favor? Roscoe asks.

Everyone raises a hand.

Fine, he continues. So here's the chant. Remit it to memory.

Wrong word, idiot, Planka says under her breath.

Roscoe glares at her, she smiles back insincerely.

The chant:

Oh father Rom and fertile Mom, ignite the bomb, incite the Mole, and from that fiery Hole the Don's shoes will be re-soled. And then the chorus: *Romper room Dump-us, Ronaldo the Bumpus, unto us a brand new Rumpus.* Repeat three times.

So fucking stupid, sighs Planka.

Just do it, says Roscoe. Oh, and one more thing. You two girls have to be naked.

Thirty-six

Brittle Snot News' live coverage of Mallory Malaise Brine addressing a politically photoshopped replica of the U.S. Congress:

Brine, dressed in bright green, across her belly a shocking reproduction of Edvard Munck's *The Scream.* She opens her mouth and begins ... unsurprisingly ... to scream:

Colleagues, coal miners, co-fabricators of republican unreality, lend me your fears. For I have come to bully Birdswell, not to appease him. Four and twenty centipedes ago, our forebrains brought forth to this continental style breakfast a new delusion, up over and beyond the people, one gas station, under the gods, myself included, with automatic weapons and plenty of spicy mustard for all.

Vigorous applause from the republican side of the chamber.

A chant erupts within the ultra right Mugwort faction:

Brine in the house, wouldn't eat a mouse, Brine on a horse, fully-clothed of course, Brine in the air, never shaves her armpit hair, Brine in a mine, dead men think she's fine, Brine in your ear, never kissed a queer, killed a liberal with a spear, and the rads all quake in fear.

Mallory continues: Many of our precious homophobic states are disappearing without a trace. Recently I travelled to the deep red core of one of our reddest regions. It was no longer there. Gone. A big fat void, filled with icy smoke and rotting MAGA miscreants. God fearing rednecks turned to scary skeletons. A serious source of our repressed desires, our unending lies ... vanished forever. And I cried: where have you gone, Ronaldo Rumpus? We await your resurrection into the dim light of an alternative rectal exam. We are your core, your legion of ghostly whores. We stand by your door, toilet paper in hand, patiently waiting for the glorious sound of your godly flush.

More applause, this time North Korean style (*vigorous, high-speed clapping, almost impossible to comprehend*)

Timmy Tube-Socks jumps up on his chair, turns his back to the democratic side, pulls down his pants and loudly farts.

Someone shouts: that moon ain't no realer than the big one in the so-called sky.

Order, demands the speaker of the house, a man feeling the strain of still possessing a functional brain. Let's all remember where we are, he pleads.

In a jar? someone barks.

Maybe on Mars? another yelps.

Inside a holo-graphic candy bar?

Camera focuses in Laura-loo Bobsmart's face. Her fake smile is radiant, her scowl, barely concealed, oozes invisible bloodlust. Her eyes, resembling an enraged rattlesnake's, glow with demonic zeal.

Green continues:

The deep end state voodoo peddlers, satan's handmaidens and the blood-guzzling demo-rats who support them, will be vanquished. Stop the squeal, school shootings ain't real, all hail the Rumpus.

Raucous fake applause, piped in over the chamber's sound system.

There you have it, says a beaming Carla Canale. Exclusively on Brittle Snot News. Nothing short of a heart-stopping, mind-numbing, life-mutilating address by Mallory Malaise Brine, rising harlot of the WAGA faction, darling of the WigWams, and quickly becoming a serious contender for the number two spot on the next presidential cricket squad. At one point in her speech, Brine waxing pathetically poetic, yet still bubbling with patriotic postmortems, calling forth the tyrannical four feathers of the nation, while sending a spine-tickling tumbleweed for that terrible thing that comes after this terrible thing. Anti-progressive boredom and stupidity is a mismanaged spectacle, Brine informs us. We must be vigilantly vile. Fight the desire to be interesting, or to do origami, or, god forbid, to say things that could be construed as reasonable.

But enough from me. Trucker Maelstrom, on loan from Screaming Meanie News, is standing by, no doubt rubbing his crotch with no small amount of glee. So, Trucker, how about it?

About my crotch-rubbing, Carla?

I think we're all well aware of your stance on that issue, Trucker.

In that case, I'll say this. The Brine speech had it all. From Shakespeare's thinly veiled pedophilia to Jack the Ripper's bloody breakfast toast to Robert E Lee's enormous ball sack. In a word, classic Malaise. Only thing missing were those hungry horse whispers, but then we can't expect everything. Summing up, and excuse my refusal to be woke, but for one brief instant I felt proud to be a pasty white boy in this great American starch factotum.

I'll gobble down a slice of white bread to that, says Carla Canale. What's that? Oh really. Well, great. Carla takes a deep breath. I've just been informed that our congressional concubine, Tracy Trump, has managed to corral Laura-loo Bobsmart. Shimmying over to you, Tracy.

Thanks, Carla. I'm standing here in the pit, as it's called, although more resembling a bubbling caldron on the edge of a constitutional abyss, but let's not shoot ourselves in the groin over semantics. Here with me, looking about as happy as a condemned woman strapped to a lethal injection table, is Laura-loo Bobsmart.

So, Congress-creature Bobsmart, what did you think of that performance by MMB?

Laura-loo's ear-to-ear smile and bulging eyes makes Tracy visibly shudder. Are you referring to Mickey Mouse Boobs?

Uh ...

Sorry, that's just one of my pet names for Malaise Brimstone ... I mean Brine.

I, uh, see. Anyway, what did you think of her speech.

Yeah, I'm pretty sure some sort of minimally intelligent artificial additive wrote it for her.

Really?

No, just kidding, of course. I loved it ... almost as much as I hated it. When Mallory opens her mouth, stuff comes out, that's for sure. Naturally, I didn't hate all of it. Certainly not as much as I've come to hate her. A long, cackling Laura-loo laugh. See how I kid around?

So, uh, you and Malaise Brine came up together, didn't you?

You mean her hanging around my neck? Do you know how heavy she is? How she never shuts up?

Uh ... kidding?

Of course. Ha Ha. Malaise is a single sex act in the speaker's private bathroom away from emerging as a defining voice of ultra-conservative unreality.

And what exactly is ...

Basically, more border walls, fewer borders, more water falls, less unisex shower stalls, excessive gun ownership, God-shaped gummy bears, strictly Bible-based marriages, the abolition of all unruly pronouns, the end of progress, once and for all, and ... did I mention the guns?

Worthy goals, for sure, says Tracy, but do you really think children should be allowed to carry lethal weapons.

Glad you asked. I'm proud to say that in my home state we've recently raised the minimum age for legal gun possession to first graders.

Wow!

I know.

Just one more thing, Laura-loo.

Anything for you, Tracy-poo.

All the recent chatter about the so-called blathers sweeping across our former American leper colony. Any comment?

Another false flag conjured by the Holly Molly-backed, deep in the peep bubble factory.

To what end, exactly?

To convince us that the facts have cracks, to render us passive through parsimony, and ultimately give us the four-wheel bum's rush into the nearest loony bin.

Well said, congress-felon Bobsmart.

My pleasure, Trudy. You know, if I wasn't the biggest hetero man-eater west of the Moose Flats Aberration, I might just slip you a tiny taste of the Laura-loo tongue.

Thirty-seven

We're facing dire straits, says a rumpled Mellmack.

Portmanteau slowly nods. Straight or gay, the dust bin of destiny is our due dessert.

The desert is making more sense by the Seconal.

We could grumble away our anti-vacation non-time in scattered pieces.

What day do you suppose it is, Portmanteau?

According to my calculations, it's approximately Tuesday a week ago next Thursday.

Remember time?

The fickle arrow.

The tremulous troubadour.

Ah, what might have been, Mellmack.

Any new readouts in the roundabout?

Entropy continues making silly faces, but I don't know enough to form a hippopotamus.

I wonder if they still offer those hippo rides at the aquarium?

When I woke up tomorrow morning it was still yesterday.

Ah, the Beatles.

Giggle, wiggle and wampum.

Based on your reversed calculus, Portmanteau, are we getting older or younger?

Hard codicils, Mellmack. I no longer have a reflection, but based upon a cursory misapprehension of your face, you'll be a hundred before the cook flips mice.

Should we attempt to reform the President, Portmanteau?

Based on my recent finger paintings, President Board-game has already turned into a pilates of rust and dust.

So who do you think is in charge?

Sorry, what?

Let me re-phrase. Whoa to the stink on a garbage scow?

Hold on, Mill Sack, I'm being rudely teleported to an attenuated dimension.

And?

I'm now convinced that the Lunar Lizard has assumed top spot on the compost heap.

Long live the Lizard, I suppose.

Just imagine.

Ah, the Beatles.

Do you suppose we're blathering out of control at this very monument, Merrimack?

We're science bugs, Porterhouse. Our finely mooned minds resist all but the most fancy-pants giblets of gibberish.

You're right, of course.

If only there was some way we could disabuse our database.

There's always a reboot?

I've always been more of a loafer person.

Is this suddenly making sense?

Don't scare me.

Maybe we only dress like scientists to elude the lawgiver.

The aliens will want to talk with us, you know.

Which came first, the aliens or the entropy?

I dreamed all this once, Portmanteau.

I weeped at your funeral, Mellmack.

And then?

You miraculously rose from the breadline.

It's starting all over again, isn't it?

As far as my smell goes, I think we're riding a wave function that refuses to crack.

Run the numbers again, says Mellmack.

Righty Oh, says Portmanteau. Ready?

As I'll never be.

Okay, red 48.

Nothing.

Black 17.

Nada.

Red 143.

I begin to wonder wonder wonder if this incessant bingo playing is truly the way forward.

Forward or back, Mellmack. Two sides of the same tenderloin.

So how would you unscramble these eggs, Portmanteau?

We have to face the factoids, my fried friend. We're stuck upon a deterministic unicycle.

Mellmack gets up and walks across the room, and at the same time remains in his chair. Portmanteau watches twenty or so Mellmacks stretch between two hypothetical points. He begins a calculation to determine exactly how many Mellmacks can exist in a single slice of existential pie. The final number is a one, followed by a thousand zeros. How many quadrillions of Mellmacks, he wonders, does it take to screw in all the lightbulbs in China?

Thirty-eight

Marsha Abernathy and Mollie Millicent enter the newly reconfigured trapezoid office holding hands. Their eyes occasionally meet, provoking smiles, the subtle licking of lips, the increased beating of hearts. Both are married, unhappily, to the sort of men who, under different circumstances, would no doubt be facing death by firing squad.

Should we tell him? Marsha wonders.

Well, says Mollie, he is the President.

But does he know he's the President? Marsha asks.

Mollie makes the *Hmm* sound, and leaves it at that.

Besides, says Marsha, he may not remember what a lesbian is.

President Birdswell is slumped forward at his desk, his forehead resting on a file displaying the *Extreme Top Secret* stamp.

One more ETS file for us to run through the shredder, says Millicent.

Marsha sighs. Mister President? Sir, can you hear me? Time to wakey wakey.

Birdswell snorts, his head jerking upwards. Oh Sharon, he says, I must have dozed off.

No Mister President, it's me, Marsha.

Really? How long have we been married, Marsha?

No Sir, you're still married to Sharon.

So you're my spicy tidbit on the side, then?

Your press secretary, actually.

Code, huh? I like it.

Sir, it's Mollie Millicent, says Mollie.

A minute ago it was Mardi Gras, wasn't it?

What's a minute ago? Mollie asks Marsha.

Marsha shrugs. No, Mister President, there are two of us.

So I'm not seeing double.

No, Sir. Also she's black, I'm white.

Like one of those cookies. What I'd give for one of those mixed race babies right about now.

And also we're lovers, Mollie shouts.

Cookie lovers? Birdswell asks. Who isn't?

No, human sexual lovers.

The three of us? Doesn't sound much like me ... but then, I have no idea who I am.

You're Moe Birdswell, President of the Unidentified States of Antarctica.

If you say so. So what's on the menu?

Well, Sir, we've discussed it with the cabinet, as well as VP Mongoose, and we all agree that it's probably time for us to abandon ship.

You know, says Birdswell, I had no idea we were even on a ship.

No, Sir, says Marsha, it's just an expression.

Oh, like two to tango.

Right.

Tricky dance that tango.

Mollie whispers to Marsha: You realize the longer this goes on, the more likely the blathering will kick in.

Marsha senses it most likely already has, but chooses to keep it bottled up.

Long story short, Sir, she says, Senator MacDougal is threatening a lizard insurrection. Senators Crust and Palsy are claiming party loyalty and backing him, even as they admit having grave doubts about the whole lounge lizard lunacy.

So, good old Glitch is finally dropping the facade, laughs Birdswell.

You knew about it, Mister President? Mollie asks.

I've seen him on more than one occasion in the Capitol gym showers, says Birdswell. Not a sight you get used to in a hurry.

The irony, Marsha snickers, is that both the WAGAs and the WIGWAMs claim the lizards are strictly in the pocket of the radical left.

A snake in your cake is worth two in the bush, says Birdswell.

In any case, Mister President, says Mollie, if MacDougal and his lizard cronies are merely the first wave of a full scale alien homestay, we need to get you to a secure location, pronto.

So we're definitely buying into the whole alien thing? Birdswell wants to know.

They're right here, says Mollie, pointing to her head.

Hard to argue with that, says Marsha.

Still, says Birdswell, I'd like to talk to Senator Windy Mayhem about all this first.

Sir, says Marsha, with respect, Mayhem spent the better part of four years with his head up the rectal cavity of Ronaldo Rumpus.

Windy never does do anything half-ass, says Birdswell.

The point is, Sir, his credibility has been completely flushed, says Marsha.

A real poopy head, in other words, adds Mollie.

That settles it, says Birdswell. Get me General Platypus on the horn. Do we still say horn?

Marsha and Millicent look at each other for an answer on the horn question. How many kinds of horn are there, they wonder. And what sort of horn could support a man the size of the borderline obese General Platypus?

Anyway, Sir, says Marsha, we regret to inform you that the General has taken the entire sixth fleet to the Canadian border to repel what he refers to as an onslaught of undead illegals and their part-time parlor maids.

And we're buying this undead thing? Birdswell asks.

Not as yet, Sir, says Millicent, but it's only a matter of time. Hey, I remembered time!

Afraid you've lost me, Birdswell tells her.

She means slime, Mister President, Marsha says.

And what about China? Birdswell wants to know.

Most of us are convinced it's not an actual place, says Marsha.

Birdswell: And all the Chinese running around?

Millicent: Most likely professional actors.

Marsha: Or crazy people staging a reenactment of World War 3.

Millicent: Or, of course, lizard lookalikes.

Birdswell: Remind me, when exactly did we fight World War 3?

Marsha: Just before the first phase of the alien subterfuge.

Birdswell: Last question before I hand in my resignation. How long was I asleep?

Marsha and Millicent: We'll let you know as soon as you wake up, Mister President.

Thirty-nine

A crowd estimated at approximately 143 maintain their position on the 9th green, directly above the site where most are convinced former President Rumpus' crypt is located. The majority of them would probably have already abandoned the vigil, especially considering the above ground temperature to be somewhere around 111 degrees Fahrenheit (no one has any idea what that would be in Centigrade), but most of them are both seriously overweight and extremely dehydrated. Not the optimal conditions in which movement, even a necessary escape, can easily occur. They have also been slowly melting for days. This runoff of human flesh, combined with the ten or so inches of globally warmed sea water overflow they are standing in, has many wondering if their continued commitment to deranged loyalty is really worth it. Making matters worse, the five hundred square mile clump of rotting seaweed that has been moving up the coast, as of this morning having breached the shoreline adjacent to the Rumpus compound, is now proceeding steadily inland.

Greta Billbasto is the first to notice it. What is that awful smell? she asks in her excessively irritating Floridian twang.

Don't know, says her husband Barney, but it stinks like that swamp behind the house, right after the septic tank exploded.

Sweet Jesus, echoes Helen, wife of Carl Dingle, owner of the nearby Carl's Doughnut Shop. It's exactly how Carl's breath smells in the morning.

If true, says Carl, why ain't you up and divorced me yet?

Cause divorce is a mortal sin, says Helen. Also, I love the free doughnuts.

Tell me something I don't know, grumbles Carl.

Well that's just about everything, cackles Helen.

Stop talking in riddles, woman, Carl snarls.

I'll tell you one thing, says Marlene Mosscrack, Helen's friend from the *500-Pound-and —Above-Large-Ladies-Club*. I'm convinced the Q-Tip-Anon-Ymous spoke to me in a daydream.

Praise the Lord, howls Helen. What tell pray, did He have to say?

That by the second Monday from the last monthly reckoning, President Rumpus will be back in the Bigfoot's Armpit, busy compiling a list of Born Again serial killers to replace all the judges on the Supreme Court.

As long as they is God-fearing, church-going murderers who oppose abortion, says Helen.

Suddenly, from across the sludge-covered fairway, a trumpet sounds. All their bleary eyes turn to see what at first appears to be a mirage; some sort of strange-looking airship floating down from the sky, sinking a foot or so into the swampy soil upon landing. A door whooshes open, and from it emerges a squat, big-boned blonde in thigh-high red waders, carrying what looks to be a small alligator.

Well thrash me with a Bible Belt, coos Greta Billbasto, but if that's not Malaise Brine, I will eat a white bread sandwich with nothing on it but this horrible stinking sea-sap.

The group really has no control over it. They begin the chant.

Malaise Brine, ain't she fine, soon to be the bride of Frankenstein.

Mallory waves her alligator, which everyone can now see is not alive, but rather stuffed, while fighting her way through a thick bubbling glob of reddish/green sludge. She seeks out a small section of higher ground, ascends its slope, spins around to face the group.

Hoo Wee, she bellows, sure smells like a radical lefty barbecue around here.

Malaise, Malaise, these are the happy days.

Brine beams, opening and closing her mouth, pretending to bite the head off the stuffed alligator.

I suspect y'all know why I'm here, she shouts.

Rumpus, bumpus, the Dom is gonna hump us.

Alive, well and back from fake news purgatory, Malaise screeches. I just got off my very smart phone, talking to none other than Romper-room Roscoe himself. I can tell you with all the sincerity of my Minnie Mouse-size heart that the reanimation of The Master is well under way.

Reanimation, save the nation ... X 3...

Malaise Brine's smarty pants phone rings. She holds up a finger for silence. 143 middle fingers rise in support.

That's super duper news, she says. Keep us upside down.

143 jaws collectively drop.

Roscoe reports the sounding of a loud and distinctively Rumpus-like fart, Malaise informs. The Dom is passing divine wind.

A collective cheer rising up through the toxic air.

Fart ... Fart ... It's a joyful start ..

Mallory, someone shouts, any plans to become the Dom's eighteenth concubine?

Let's just say I'm near the top of a very short hit list.

Whoops and squeals.

More importantly, shouts Brine, we are on the verge. The left is set to lose. This repugnant sludge? We all know the source, right? The deep state outhouse, of course. Seaweed sushi and liberal poopy. How do I know we'll win this war?

She lifts aloft the alligator, shakes it like an angry babysitter abusing an infant child.

Because the Lizard People are finally with us. Old geezer Glitch MacDougal has finally seen the light. We have the right to fight, day or night. The aliens, too, have come over to our side. As we speak, their turd-shaped ships patrol our borders, vaporizing all illegals attempting to cross. Fake President Birdswell has already abandoned the Bigfoot's Boner.

Thick-limbed clapping and ponderous hand-waving; puddles of sweat forming, baby tadpoles spring to life within them. It's a clear sign. The latest miracle of Merry Legoland.

God is with us, oozes Marlene Mosscrack.

God's in my bed ... He lives in my head ... He brings back the dead

Helen Dingle appears to swoon. Five people shift their massive body weight, enveloping her.

Mallory's phone pings. She opens it, finds a video of Planka Moremoney and half-sister Tammy, naked, jumping up and down in front of what must be The Dom's Holy Hideaway. She stares with brittle envy at Planka's nudity. All of it unreal, she reminds herself. The best fake boobs and butt money can buy. She smiles maliciously, resends the video to Laura-loo Bobsmart.

Something distracts the crowd - a noise, a smell, a vision of new age hell? - forcing their heads to turn back towards the mysterious flying machine in which Malaise Brine arrived. They stare as the door opens a second time, emerging from within what appears to be a perfect copy of Mallory Malaise, with the singular exception that this Mallory Malaise has two distinct heads. A collective gasp, followed by a parched gulp, from the group, several of whom begin muttering prayers while maniacally rubbing their eyes.

They begin to sing:

Our eyes have seen the coming of a second Mallory Malaise
Now she has two heads and we are awestruck and amazed
We will light the torches and the world will be ablaze
Her teeth keep gnashing on

The two-headed Brine crosses the molten 11th fairway, slithers up the hill, where once Jack (*Rumpus*) assaulted Jill (*waitress at the Merry Legoland snack bar*), then merges into the original one-headed Brine. For an instant this composite Brine has three heads ... then two ... then just the one. Mallory Malaise opens her mouth and issues a very loud burp.

At the risk of outing herself as a heretical Catholic, Greta Billbasto diligently crosses herself.

Forty

One tenth of a mile below the ground, a winded Planka sits with her back to the sarcophagus, haphazardly attempting to conceal her nudity. A naked Tammy is bent over and gasping for air. Egbert stands behind her, making no effort to avert his gaze. His half-sister's ass is the best thing he's seen in he can't remember the name of that tune.

What I'd like to know, cries Roscoe, is why you've all stopped?

I'll tell you why, says Planka. Because nothing's happening and you're a fucking idiot.

Nothing, Planka? We all heard that fart.

We herd *a* fart, she says. Almost certainly Egbert's.

No, counters Roscoe. That fart was muffled, clearly having to fight its way through several heavy layers to reach us.

Have you seen what Egbert's wearing? Planka asks.

Egbert, did you fart? Roscoe asks.

I don't know, says Egbert. I fart so much I don't even notice it anymore.

Doesn't matter, says Roscoe. That was definitely not an Egbert fart.

Maybe hers, then, says Planka, nodding in the direction of Tammy.

Screw you, Planka, Tammy tells her. Think I'd know if I farted.

In the same way you'd know if Egbert was staring at your bare ass for the past ten ... whatever those things are called?

Millennium bugs, as I recall, says Roscoe.

I'm also pretty sure I saw a large crawly thing behind Daddy's boxcar, says Tammy.

You know, says Planka, the longer we stay down here, the dumber you three get.

None of us are walking outta her geniuses, says Roscoe, but still, we can't just give up.

I can, Planka tells him.

And I'm not giving you any more blood, says Tammy.

Nobody wants your fucking weird green blood, Roscoe tells her. It's Planka's blood we need, which by the way was the original plan.

Fuck your original plan, Planka hisses, and while you're at it, fuck yourself.

Hey, says Egbert, Tammy has a bumpy butthole.

So stop staring at it, Tammy whines.

So stop bending over like that, Planka tells Tammy.

Oh Yeah, snaps Tammy. Well at least I don't shave my pubescents.

Trust me, says Planka, we noticed.

You think the world is still up there? Egbert asks, pointing straight up.

What's the world? Tammy wonders.

I'll call you when I get there and let you know, says Planka, beginning to search for her clothes.

Of course, Roscoe cries, rifling through one of the sacred texts - i.e. comic books - it was never about the blood.

Please don't say we have to climb up there and make pee pee on Daddy, says Tammy.

As much as he'd like that, says Planka.

No one's peeing on Daddy, Roscoe tells them. But you two, he says, indicating Planka and Tammy, have to climb up there and have sex.

Sex with Planka? Tammy gulps breathlessly. Another girl, my half-sister, no less? I'm so disgusted by the thought, I can almost hardly wait.

Okay, that's it, says Planka, now back in her minimalist lacy black underwear. She grabs her bag, reaches inside and pulls out the gold-plated 9mm pistol Morty had bought her for Valentine's Day.

Holy shit, Planka, screams Egbert, attempting to vanish inside his pelts.

***

Several popping sounds from beneath the ground attract the rapidly diminishing attention of the group above.

What is heaven's maiden name was that? Helen Dingle exclaims.

More farts? Marlene Mosscrack wonders.

Even better, says Malaise Brine. It's the start of the rewind, the unclipping of the queen's corset, Planka's full-frontal reveal, the edge of nowhere, the heebees and the jeebees, the holy comeuppance, the first and the last, the blast from the past, the dumb face of Bobsmart, the sweet decay of my own vampire fangs, the ...

The crowd of 142 (one man in the back has sadly given up the ghost) is held rapt, breathless, their brains very close to bursting into flame.

Please, pleads a gasping Greta Billbasto.

We beseech thee, wails Helen Dingle, dropping to her knees, sinking down to her waist in a mixture of fuming seaweed and volatile swamp water.

Brine does a little dance, her waders squeaking.

They begin meekly chanting:

Mallory Malaise, put us in a daze, dropped us in a maze, all doughnuts should be honey-glazed ...

Forty-one

The attention of Jane, Mickelmoose, et al, is diverted by a whooshing-whirring noise from above. Emerging from an oblong cloud cluster an oddly shaped metallic caboose suspended beneath long, rotating thingamabobs.

Santini draws his weapon, aiming it at what he has no doubt is an unidentified flying objection.

Jane notices, screams at him. Hold your fire, numb nuts.

Harsh, mutters Mickelmoose, but long overdue.

Santini's expression can best be described as incredulous, if only anyone had any faith that such a word exists. Perhaps it's escaped your retention, he says to Jane, but we are under attack.

Talk about getting gobsmacked, says Mickelmoose.

I lost my virginity in a haystack, says Reindeer.

The mysterious vehicle touches down next to one of the patrol cars. The door opens and a woman jumps out, followed by a second woman and a man carrying a ... *this word also appears to have been misplaced.* They approach the four officers.

Santini again draws his weapon; this time Mickelmoose does as well.

Halt, someone shouts. Who goes there?

The first woman disregards the order to halt, continues her approach. She appears to be of Asian descent.

Try freeze, Mickelmoose suggests.

Why freeze? Santini asks. It's practically the middle of Somerset Maugham.

Freeze happens to be the universal antidote, says Mickelmoose.

Hi, the woman says. Candace Wong, B.S. News.

Just great, snarls Santini, the media muddle dusters.

The public sleepwalkers do have a right to know, says Reindeer.

Sergeant Jankowitz, says Jane, offering her hand to Candace Wong.

Hey, says Mickelmoose, that weirdo contraption from which you just mysteriously materialized, might one call that a ... bird?

Sure, Candace tells him, I guess it's been called that.

Yeah, says Santini, but on what frigging planet?

That's enough, Jane says. You three go mismanage the barrier reef.

Which three? Mickelmoose asks. Us three, or them three?

You three, Jane points at Mickelmoose, Santini and Reindeer; aka The Three Stooges, she adds.

Listen, Sergeant, says Candace, hope we're not stepping on anyone's toes here.

Jane glances down at her feet, shakes her head.

I'm actually surprised they're are only four of you, continues Candace. I mean, you do know what coming this way, right?

Jane has no idea what's coming this way, but says, we have been receiving a steady stream of top of the line show and tell.

So you know, Candace says.

Oh, says Jane, we know. Do you know?

Obviously not like you know, says Candace.

I know, Jane agrees, though I wouldn't mind knowing what you do know.

Can't ever know too much, too soon, I suppose, says Candace.

Jane finds herself staring at Candace Wong's mouth, wondering what a kiss would be like and, assuming the female reporter is agreeable, whether or not she'll tell Jenna.

We just flew over the ... uh ... mass, for lack of a better word.

And this mass, as you call it, approximately how large would you say it is?

Uh, very.

Very?

Very Very.

And these are people, more or less, right?

Hard to say. Sometimes you can see what appears to be individual humanoids, sometimes they all seem to meld together into a single vibratory clump of decaying anti-matter.

Precisely what our idiosyncratic intel suggests.

So, says Candace, are you currently seeing anyone?

Well, says Jane, I'm currently seeing you, but only because I'm looking right at you.

I'll take that as a no, then, says Candace.

I know I would, says Jane.

Would you like to see the tape? Candace asks.

Don't tell me, Jane laughs. You were young, wild, rebelling against the system; that porno tape you made just sort of materialized out of the blue.

I like the way your minefield meanders, Candace tells her.

No doubt you've also noticed my noodles, Jane says.

Actually, we stopped for snacks earlier.

Earlier? Jane wonders. Possibly some TV celebrity jargon?

Anyway, says Candace, care to step aboard my flying carpet?

Should I continue recording, Ms. Wong? the cameraman asks.

You've been recording this whole time? Candace irritably inquires.

Sort of what I do, he says. All I do, actually.

Well, go over there by The Three Stooges, she tells him. Shoot them.

You can use my gun if you don't have your own, Jane tells him.

I've always been more of an Abbott and Costello man myself, he replies.

What about me? the other member of Candace's team asks.

I'm not even sure who you are, the cameraman tells her.

Candace shoves him in the direction of the invisible barrier.

You'd better come with us, Brenda, she says.

Jane can't help imagining the three of them actually coming together. Wasn't that a Beatles song? Was it really about mutually spontaneous lesbian orgasms?

As long as you two don't think three's a crowd, says Brenda.

When is a crowd not a crowd? Candace wonders.

When it's an unidentified and potentially dangerous mass? Jane guesses.

Mickelmoose glances over at the females, observes Jane and the other two walk towards what could very well be the last bird on Earth, and at the same time remain exactly where they are; like ghost trails being stretched across extra-dimensional sidecars, shivering phantoms at an all night bird watching party. He has no idea what any of this means, but is convinced he must be gazing into the afterlife.

Finally I understand, he weeps out loud. Death is not the end.

As Jane ascends the metallic stairs of the alien ship, she glances back at her three brothers in blue. Although the prospect of being related to any of these men sends a metaphorical switchblade slicing through her large intestine. And as she gazes, she observes Santini and Reindeer ascend into the air. They are smiling, holding hands, like a pair of make believe angels who were only pretending to be lowlife morons on Earth.

***

Burr feels his entire body catch fire. He also feels it turn to ice. Burning in ice, freezing in fire. Life, he thinks, is paradox ... is a pair of socks ... a parrot in a box ... an ancient clock.

My mind's a whirring turbine, he tells himself ... a shattered singularity. Wait, he thinks, is that what all this is about? The singularity? Much blathered about, rarely gobbled by fiendish entities. Speaking of entities, unsavory and lacking in all personal hygiene, Bob the Blob continues to dog him like a lingering nightmare. Is it possible that Bob's the singularity? The impossible and repugnant life form that knows all and also nothing at all?

Hey, Goldilocks, Bob groans into Burr's still functional ear, deep thought always reverberates to naught. Nothing but nothing equals a little placenta I like to call Nerve-Anna.

Who are you, Burr asks, Bob the Buddhist?

Was born Bill the Baptist, oozes Bob.

Don't forget Pete the Presbyterian, says Burr. Or possibly Tom the Taoist.

Knew you was a commie sympathizer the first smell I got of ya, says Bob.

Listen Bob, what's your deal?

Keep pressing me, Mary Jane, and I'll make you squeal.

The mass hits a bump in the road, an elongated shudder vibrating through it, like an angry shock wave sent up from the center of the earth.

Wait, wonders Burr, can a flat earth have a center?

Only if it's a one-dimensional point, offers a drooling Bob.

Still, there is a sudden sense of infinity; at the same time, the inevitable ending of all things. What will be, won't.

Burr concludes that fate can only be revealed in frightening fairy tales. If only there was enough ... he struggles for the word, reasonably sure it once upon a star started with a T.

Bob, he says, if I say the letter T, what do you say?

Bob snorts. Telltale Heart, Tegucigalpa, Teratophobia, Tachythanatous ...

Burr's pretty sure none of those are the word he's looking for. Nor could he have guessed that Bob would have come up with these words, if they even are words. Who is Bob, anyway? Is he Bob, the poet philosopher from Central America? Bob, the Devil in a blue dress? Bob, the inhuman cog in this vast riddle machine? Maybe Bob is merely a figment of his imagination, the worst possible made up person with whom to walk forever across the surface of a planet.

For whom the bell tolls, echos Bob the Blob.

Burr's mind briefly wanders to the girl with no name waiting for him in a marginal location called Ida Ho. A Chinese American girl, possibly, with one slender Asian arm down the front of her pants, murmuring in the lost language of a billion ghosts, waiting for the return of her itinerant lover, Bob.

No, not Bob, Burr screams. Burr. Burr, Burr, Burr.

Starting to bore me, Burt, says Bob. I'll swallow you hole and have your surviving relatives worship me as the Holy Burb, complete with subatomic subtitles.

Forty-two

The earth quivers and roils beneath their feet. Jets of hot air spew from eyeball-size openings in the mantlepiece. Santini begins recklessly firing into the ground. Reindeer starts crying; Mickelmoose pulls him close in an embrace. Candace is live, on air, clearly on thin ice. The public, what remains of it, wants assurances. Jane is not sure how to proceed. She realizes that she's left her bra in the brass bunker. Brenda is nowhere to be found. Is it possible that either she or Candace killed Brenda is a fit of jealous tomfoolery?

Can you hear me, sperm bank? Candace screams into her microphone.

Irritating static returns through her earpiece.

At least I hope this gets recorded for posterity, says Candace.

Jane contemplates Candace's posterity, so slim yet so curvaceous, both taut and pulpy, reminiscent of a Tegucigalpa tangerine.

Candace beckons her over.

Okay, Candace, the voice of Bright Silversperm crackles, think we've got you now.

Great, Sliver Germ, says Candace. I'm here on the edge of somewhere-or-other, at what's being described as the last human aberration, the broken arrow end zone, if you will. Next to me is Sergeant Jane *sexy little slut* Jankowitz, with whom I've just had a rumble-bumble in the low-earth-orbiting Winnebago...

Sorry, Canned Mace, says Bright, lost that last bit.

So Sergeant, says Candace, can you tell our audience what, in your professional opinion, is happening here?

Gee whiz, Candace, says Jane, what isn't happening here? We've got love, sex, death rattles, robot subversion, bare butts, lost underwear, a glaring lack of personal growth, workplace regret and a whole lot of nothing else. Oh, and we also have an actual reindeer on site.

Sorry, statics Bright. Did someone say it's raining deer?

Hope you like your venison bruised and bloody, Blight, says Candace.

I've always preferred a horse of a different color, Candace, says Bright.

Candace gives him the finger.

Sorry, he says, couldn't quite see what you're pointing at.

What about your men, Sergeant? Candace asks. Can you fill us in on what they're up to?

Well, Candace, as you can see, one of my officers, Santini, the poster boy of corrupt fops, has lost his fucking mind. The other two, Moose Breath and Rain Man, appear to be hot and heavy making out. Desperate rhymes breed hopeless wrecks, as the saying goes.

And the barrier?

It's our last line of pretense, Candace.

And beyond that?

Uh, the great blue yonder, the big black hole in an even bigger fishbowl, the ultimate cosmic wax job, the fickle fungus of fatalists?

Jane Jankowitz, coos Candace, postal worker as well as poet.

Jane blushes, wishes she and Candace were back in the spaceship.

Through the mist comes a sniveling, trembling Brenda, wearing only panties and bra. Jane is certain the bra Brenda's got on is hers. Mickelmoose takes one long look at Brenda, pushes Reindeer over the barrier and begins walking slowly, arms outstretched, towards her. Brenda screams, the sound flying upwards, bouncing off thick metallic-tasting clouds and ricocheting back to earth.

They told us Frankenstein's monster wasn't real, Brenda wails, but they lied.

Jane considers shooting Mickelmoose, wonders if Jenna will notice her missing bra, or the bite marks on her breasts, or, for that matter, the whip marks on her things and buttocks. Low lighting is obviously the key, she tells herself.

And then ...

... a terrible, teeth-rattling wail from across the great divide, strange peekaboos of light riddle the sky, the obscure lingo-chattering of what could very well be the new Lizard Oligarchs of Planet Mirthless. Just then, above, a parting of cloud, a large, glowing white sphere emerges. Some call it Moon; so obviously unreal it appears absolutely real. On both sides of the Mason-Dixon, all eyes are cranked skywards.

Okay, says Jane, if anyone has anything to wipe, now's your chance.

***

Burr realizes that he and Bob are all of a sudden sharing several strategic body parts; the sensation is somewhat less than pleasurable. Around them, what's left of humanity's dregs, now an undifferentiated and fetid-smelling mass, issues a long-winded moan.

If I have to pee, Burr wonders, whose pecker will I be pulling out to do it with?

Don't matter, says Bob, the crustacean clairvoyant. We no longer exist, and if we don't exist, you don't need to piss.

Oh yeah, says Burr. Tell that to our mutual pecker.

Up ahead, or possibly behind, a long shimmering edge; a straight line of burning fossil fuels and the charred remains of the unfaithful. In Burr's decomposing mind, it stretches all the way back to the moment of cosmic desecration.

Is that ..?

Edge of the whirlwind, says Bob.

So the Earth really is ..?

As a pancake.

Will you hold me? a teary Burr asks.

Rather knife you in various vital organs, Bob growls.

Burr sees himself as he was, as he will be, an endless loop running through the three stages of existential grief: *nothing, maybe something, no, definitely nothing.*

Different choices rarely lead to different outcomes, says a weary Burr.

Save the sermon, Sally, and move it, grunts Bob. We've got a helluva tumble ahead of us.

Forty-three

Mallory Malaise Brine stands before her bedroom mirror, trying to make sense of what's she's looking at. A partially fragmented face, one drooping eyeball, a nose bent almost in half; resembling something that godless pervert Pablo Pistachio might have painted in one of his drug-infested, all-night sex stupors.

What went wrong? is what she'd like to know. The Waga Wigwams, the Mugworts, the stay at home alcoholic moms and their abusive husbands working menial jobs, the Loud boys and the White Boy Toy Brigade, the heavily-armed Hitler home-schoolers, the fatties and the furious, the dumb and the even dumber, all waiting for that prophesied moment: the great rising of The Don. President Ronaldo Rumpus boring his way upwards, rejuvenated, revisited, re-rectified, emerging proud, barely a rotting corpse, reclaiming his God-given place as ruler of the Everything and the Everywhere.

She had waited as long as she could. Perched atop The Don's favorite tee, her chubby hand outstretched, waiting to ascend with The Man/God of money-filled goodie bags. With the stagnant waters rising, the toxic sea guck expanding exponentially, she had excused herself, fibbed, something about the early arrival of her period, or was it an early appointment with her Biblical blasphemy class? The people had continued to chant, singing her name, even as they slowly sank beneath the muck and the mire. A few visible hands, mostly of those not wheelchair-bound, slowly waving, as her rented alien shuttle rose into a turbulent cone of foul Floridian air.

I will return, she had whinnied over the ships built-in sound system.

She knew she never would. She'd sensed an ending that could never be expressed. Like having to behave rationally. It was just never gonna happen.

Beside her stands Laura-loo Bobsmart, trying to commiserate, secretly savoring Malloy's misery.

You can't blame yourself, Laura-loo tells her, as she begins to wrap Malaise Brine's naked body in the off-white gauze of mummification. She is working from the neck down, leaving the head of the beast for last.

You'll make such a yummy mummy, Laura-loo says, wrapping a second layer around Brine's already sagging breasts. Goodbye sad boobs, she whispers.

In a dream, Malaise Brine had seen herself as the mummified bride being carried on the shoulders of her brain-impaired colleagues into the crypt, to the cheers of a select few among her most deranged followers, finally lowered into the Don's tomb. She the Princess of Endless Palaver, he the Prince of Pugnacious Parsimony; her chockfull-of - crazy pandora's box to his hamburger-fueled narcissistic numb-scullery.

Something doesn't feel right, Malaise tells Laura-loo.

It's probably your bush, says Laura-loo. How long has it been since you trimmed this thing?

Do you suppose the mummy's curse is real? Malaise asks.

You're barely half a mummy, and I feel cursed just standing here with you, says Laura-loo. So, yes, I guess.

We might have been lesbian lovers in college, says Malaise.

Except neither of us went to college, Laura-loo reminds her.

Will you kiss me once, Laura-loo, before you mummify my head?

Depends how much cash you've got in your wallet, Laura-loo tells her.

You've always looked down on me, Bobsmart, Mallory sobs.

Only because I'm a political princess who floats on a puffy cloud of pure privilege, says Laura-loo.

And carries a gun.

Even I can't always get by on good looks alone.

I know, says Malaise, sometimes you have to shoot first, try your best to look pretty later.

Listen, says Laura-loo, would it make you feel better if I trimmed your bush for you?

Mallory Malaise Brine has to think long and hard about this. No other woman has ever touched this area of her body. Particularly some smug, slim-hipped floozy like Laura-loo Bobsmart. But then what's the point of continuing to pretend to have principles?Ronaldo Rumpus has abandoned us. The world is certainly finished.

With a deep sigh, Malaise Brine says ... I think the scissors are in the cabinet about the bathroom sink.

A long guffaw from Laura-loo. I was thinking garden hedge clippers, she says. But sure, let's start with the scissors, and see where it takes us.

I hate your guts, Bobsmart, sighs Malaise.

Not nearly as much as I hate yours, Brine, Laura-loo replies.

Noted, says Brine. Now where did we land on that kiss?

Also by William Leigh

Females Ascending
Jupiter Roars

The Novella Experiment
Brain-damaged America

Standalone
Cannibals Don't Inhale
The Cutest Little Demon in Town
Beautiful Assassins